THE NEW BIZAF
PR

GENOCIDE ON THE INFINITE EXPRESS

KEVIN SWEENEY

ERASERHEAD PRESS
PORTLAND, OREGON

ERASERHEAD PRESS
P.O. BOX 10065
PORTLAND, OR 97296

www.eraserheadpress.com
facebook/eraserheadpress

ISBN: 978-1-62105-292-0
Copyright © 2019 by Kevin Sweeney
Cover design copyright © 2019 Eraserhead Press

Printed in the USA.

One beginning and one ending for a book was a thing I did not agree with. A good book may have three openings entirely dissimilar and inter-related only in the prescience of the author, or for that matter one hundred times as many endings.

At Swim-Two-Birds
Flann O'Brien

I
ME

CORPSES everywhere, not all of them human, but all of them me.

Not that I knew who I was. Or where I was.

Had I just awoken? I didn't think so. I was standing up. You don't just wake up already standing. I didn't feel as though I'd been sleeping. I was just suddenly there, and my very first impression of my surroundings was to note all the dead bodies.

That was the first impression. The second was that not all of them were human. My third impression, and probably the strangest, was that even though they were dead, and even though they were not human, they were all somehow me.

My first thought; corpses everywhere, not all of them human, but all of them me.

Was that my very first thought? I mean, ever? A strange idea struck me; I had no clue who or where I was not simply because I did not remember, but that because I had never known. Not an amnesiac, but freshly minted.

Like I had just been switched on. Like a robot.

I touched my face, my arms, my chest. I wasn't a robot. At least I didn't think I was. I was made of flesh, I had skin and hair. But maybe they were artificial. I thought about gouging my flesh, to see if I would bleed, but then I thought that if my creators had gone to the trouble of giving me realistic skin and hair they may have filled my artificial veins with artificial blood. It seemed logical, and more so when I slid my hands down the front of my trousers to find that I had genitals.

All this made sense, if you wanted to make a robot that didn't know it was a robot, and you didn't ever want it to find out. Make it so human that there was no way of telling man from machine.

I was a robot.

No. I wasn't. I didn't feel like a robot. But then… how did I know what being a robot would feel like anyway? Also, wouldn't I be programmed to feel like I didn't feel like I was a robot?

I shook my head, trying to free myself from this train of thought that threatened to start winding around itself, swallowing its own stupid tail. I decided it didn't matter if I was or was not a robot. I turned my attention outward again, to my surroundings.

Some of the corpses had fallen out of their seats to sprawl in the aisle, or were slumped across each other, whilst others could almost have been napping upright. If it weren't for the obvious fatal wounds I might have tried to rouse one or two of them, but the slashed throats, the smashed skulls, the laps full of intestines, all spoke eloquently that nobody was nodding.

I was stood in the aisle between ranks of seats, black molded plastic bolted to the brushed steel floor, two apiece on either side, in a narrow corridor lit by recessed strip lighting above. It was like being in an incredibly primitive train carriage, everything stripped back to the absolute bare minimum, more a token symbol of a train carriage. The steel walls had windows in them, furthering the impression of being on some stripped back form of public transport, but there was only blackness beyond. The blackness beyond meant that the glass acted as a kind of mirror, and I could see myself and take stock.

I was a man, tall, with a thin beard and swept back black hair. I was wearing black trousers and a deep blue long sleeved shirt, tucked in; my top two buttons were open to show I was wearing a white T-shirt underneath. My face bore an unmistakable family resemblance to every other face I could see, and in some cases, was virtually identical, save for minor variations. Again, save for minor variations, they were dressed in the same manner as me.

The variations were all cosmetic. The man I saw reflected in the glass had a thin beard. Many of these others also had beards, but none was trimmed or styled in the same way as my own. Here a goatee, there a soul patch, and here again great muttonchops like fluffy wings. Moustaches were short and clipped into toothbrushes, or extravagantly waxed into great spiraling curlicues. Some of the beards I saw were sprinkled with gray hairs, whilst others were clearly dyed. I saw blue beards and pink beards, and I saw a purple and gold beard.

But then again, not every corpse had facial hair, and the variations that marked them as different from one another varied.

Hairstyles were different. Mine was short and swept back. Others were worn long, in dreadlocks, decorated with oily feathers. Some of the corpses were completely shaved, whilst others had bi-hawks.

Other variations were not cosmetic by choice, but rather the marks of chance. Some had moles; just below their hairline, to the left of their philtrum, at the corner of their eyes. Some had scars, for the most part old and healed, white and shiny, but others were fresher; animal claws had raked cheeks, knives had carved obscenities into foreheads. One of my faces had notches cut out of both his ears, and another had a ragged nostril like a nose piercing had been ripped out with pliers.

During my assessment of these dead variations of myself I had slowly begun to pace along the aisle, stepping over any bodies that sprawled across my path. Whilst I was mentally cataloging the differences, I also noticed that no matter what the manner of death had been -stabbed, shot, bludgeoned, throttled, poisoned- there was no sign of the instruments used. It was only after I consciously acknowledged that I had been looking for these weapons that the reason for my search made itself clear in my mind; I was looking for a way to defend myself.

Having stated the situation to myself I was suddenly afraid, and quickly looked in both directions, back the way I came, and forward. Everything was still. I saw no way there could be an ambush, and I certainly would not be rushed upon, because even though the only thing I could compare my surroundings to was as a kind of cypher of a train carriage, there was no sign of an end in sight, no doors to indicate the end of one carriage before you entered the next; both forwards and backwards, the ranks of seats and their dead occupants receded beyond sight.

II
MOVING

I was not yet tired, I was not yet hungry, I was not yet thirsty, I did not yet need to piss or shit. The air smelled of blood, but only faintly. The temperature was a little cold.

As I had been moving without thinking, my attention wholly upon discerning the differences between all these other versions of myself, I was no longer certain where I had started. I could no longer place exactly where I had found myself suddenly standing self-aware in this...

Train.

I had settled on that as the default image of what to compare this strange place, so I decided to call it that. I was in a strange train of seemingly endless length.

Having settled this, I found myself wondering how I knew what a train was.

Seeming to lack any personal experience -I certainly had no memory- how did I know what a train was? I tried to picture one in my head, and found I couldn't. I had no reference point to be able to say, "I came from this certain place, and in this certain place I saw a train." Even if I had only done so once, that would be enough. But no, there was no memory to make the comparison, I just knew what a train was, or at least what the inside of one of its carriages was like. There was something in my head that told me a train had specific attributes, and if I found myself able to list those attributes in my immediate surroundings, then those surroundings must be a train carriage. Or at least, I could call them that for the sake of convenience.

The narrow confines.

The seats placed so.

The windows, even though they looked out at nothing, or at least, looked out at blackness.

I took stock again.

I was not tired, I was not hungry, I was not thirsty, I did not need to piss or shit. The air smelled of blood, but only faintly. The temperature was a little cold.

Emotionally, I discovered, I only felt one thing; curiosity. I was capable of other emotions, because I had felt fear when I realized that I was looking for a weapon, fear that had made me suddenly appraise my surroundings for immediate threats. Also, I had felt a mild disgust when looking at some of the more violently deranged corpses. I wasn't a robot, I decided, not if I felt fear for myself, not if I felt queasy at the sight of eyes forced from their sockets by exploded brain matter, the skull caved in from above causing its contents to be forced out.

So, what came next? I needed a purpose, but I had

no particular need to fulfill. I did not need to locate a place to rest, or substance to eat or drink. I didn't need to secure privacy to void bladder or bowels.

Curiosity was my only drive. I had been looking for a weapon, and I understood that was to defend myself, but only as an exercise in logic; all these other versions of me were dead, so it made sense that somebody, or several of them, needed to exist to create these corpses. My basic animal needs did not need to be met, but instinct had driven me to coolly and unconsciously weigh the situation and arrive at the conclusion that I needed to defend myself. But then I had appraised my situation and reasoned that I was in no immediate danger. I did not wish to find a safe place.

So, that only left curiosity.

I decided to explore. I would continue moving in the direction I had established, if for no more good reason then I had already started that way. I would call it going forward, travelling *up* the length of the infinite express, and if I decided for whatever reason to reverse myself, I would be going back, travelling *down* the length again.

By exploring, perhaps, I would answer the basic questions of who I was, where I was, and why. And thinking this, I felt another emotion; excitement.

I began to walk, still taking care to step over any bodies which had fallen in the aisle. I only idly noted the variations in all the other versions of me that I passed, because instead I was looking for variations in the substance of the space around me.

I looked left and right at the bolted down, molded plastic chairs, looking to see if the seats were numbered.

They were not. The floor and walls and ceiling were all the same material, brushed steel, but seemingly all of one piece. There was no sign of welded plates or rivets. The recessed strip lighting above me was a uniform, illuminating bar of white light. The windows were uniformly the same length, about the space of three ranks of seating before there was a gap of one set of seating before the next window.

I thought about counting seats or windows to chart my progress, but realized that there was probably no point in doing so. I had a direction and I was motivated, tallying my progress would be superfluous, as well as futile, given that I had nothing to reckon it against; perhaps if I wore a watch and could say that I passed a dozen windows in a minute, then I could extrapolate the distance covered in an hour, and so determine my rate of progress. But I couldn't see why I would want or need to, and more to the point, I had no watch.

III
HER

AHEAD of me stretched the train into forever.

I could not place exactly when the change occurred, and not only because I lacked a watch or any means to gauge time, but because I believe it happened gradually, by small increments. By the time I was conscious of any difference it had already become the status quo.

At first, I was only aware that some change had occurred, not what the nature of the change was. It was hard to define, and yet I felt it acutely. I had been moving forward for some time, and had abandoned trying to step over the fallen corpses after reaching a length of the aisle in which the falls completely covered the steel floor, so that I had no choice but to walk across backs and chests as if they were stepping stones. The unspoken taboo broken, I no longer minded treading on the bodies, and this nonchalance was probably what made me unaware of the change even as it happened.

The notion that something was different became

so strong in me that I stopped my progress and forced myself to think it through.

The pattern of the train had not changed. The floor and walls and ceiling were still unblemished steel; the seats were the same black plastic; the view beyond the windows was still blackness.

This meant the change must have happened to the corpses.

I turned and slowly examined each one, mentally comparing them to the hundreds I had already had a chance to study as I had walked up the length of the train. Each of them was still obviously me; the set and spacing of my facial features and the general attire -blue shirt, white T-shirt, black trousers- were the same, or at least, were the same with those minor variations that made each corpse unique; the varying facial hair, the hairstyles, the scars, the placement of moles.

So, what had changed about them?

The answer was both obvious and subtle. The variations between them were no longer purely cosmetic, but more fundamental. I thought of these as major variations. The sizes of the corpses were an example; here was a giant, easily over seven-foot-tall, a gangling figure that lolled over the seat behind with his throat cut, and there was a dwarf, tumbled to the ground like a discarded toy. Not only were there vast differences in limb length, but also mass; at one point three rows of seating were packed with obese variations of me, chest flesh straining the buttons of their shirts, bellies squashed up against the seats in front. There were muscular figures and there were skeletal figures, and all body types in between.

Another major variation that occurred amongst the many dead versions of me was age. At first, I assumed that a tiny figure close at hand was simply another dwarf, but then I gave it closer scrutiny and realized that it was, in fact, a version of me as a child. The clothing was the same uniform of blue shirt, white T-shirt, and black trousers, but in toddler-sized clothing. The corpse must have been only three or four years old. Its eyes were wide open and bloodshot; the burst blood vessels and the purple-black bruises around the throat testified that it had been throttled to death.

Examining others, I saw that an entire span of years was represented. There were versions of me that ranged in age from childhood to middle age to drooling senility. Smooth skin to wrinkled skin, thick black hair to wispy white strands.

I didn't know what to make of this discovery of more radical differences between the corpses. What did it mean? Did it have to have meaning? From a practical point of view, I did not see how the knowledge could benefit me; the situation was what it was. The fact that further back the way I had come, the corpse's differences were small and largely cosmetic, and that now they were larger and… more permanent? That wasn't quite the word I wanted, but it would suffice… seemingly had no bearing on my plight. I was no better off or worse off, as far as I could tell, for my observation.

Having no better option, I resumed my original purpose of moving forward. I supposed that I could take the major variations between the dead bodies as a sign of progress, but failed to convince myself that such was the case.

I have no way of knowing how long it was or how far I travelled before I came upon the female version of me.

I had resolved to be more vigilant. The change in the nature of the corpses had taken me by surprise, even if, paradoxically, it had been a subtle process. So, it was another paradox that at the moment that I had resolved to be more vigilant that I should be taken by surprise.

She was another version of me, but the first to be a different gender. We could have been fraternal twins; the female me wore the standard uniform of black trousers, white T-shirt, and a blue shirt. Her face was mine but feminized, lips fuller, hair longer. My bone structure fitted her well, and I gauged that she was good-looking, though it was her figure that was most remarkable. The trousers she wore were filled with long shapely legs and her shirt was unbuttoned to her navel to make room for the enormous globes of her breasts; these stretched out the white T-shirt to show a deep cleavage, and exposed her collar bones, on the right of which was a small brown mole.

I unbuttoned my own shirt and pulled out the collar of my own T-shirt, and found the exact same mole.

These observations so fully preoccupied my attention that I failed to notice the fact that her gender was not the only major distinction between her and all the other versions of me. This second major difference was the lack of any signs of violence done to her.

I leaned closer to sweep her long black hair back, thinking to find a bullet hole in her temple, and she screamed.

IV
WE

.

THE me that was female explained why she had pretended to be dead.

"I heard you coming and I panicked," she said. "I thought anybody else who was alive must have, y'know, been the one who did all the killing. I tried to remain as still as I could, so I'd look like just another body… but when you got to where I was you stopped and you kept staring…"

"Because you were the first female version of me I'd come across," I said.

Her eyes narrowed a little and her head tilted slightly.

"Oh? Is that right? I thought you were just getting a good scoop at my boobs," she said. Another thought took her. "And what do you mean by a female version of you?"

We were stood in the aisle facing one another. After we had both recovered from the initial shock -my alarm at her screaming at me; her fear that I was going to murder her- she had stood up so she could appraise me and we could converse on equal footing.

I explained.

"Every corpse on this train seems to be a version of me, though each is different. But so far, no matter how many or how major the differences have been, the bodies have all been male. That was why I was so interested in you."

"And how exactly do you know that they are all versions of you, like clones or copies or something?" she asked, her chin tilting up defiantly. "How do you know that they aren't all clones of me? And you too, you could be a clone of me as well."

"I don't know that," I admitted. "I suppose they could, myself included, in fact be different versions of you. There are no facts to point to either being the truth. Or neither, I suppose."

This admission seemed to mollify her.

"So, what's your name?" she asked.

"I don't know," I said.

"You don't know?"

"No."

"Where are you from?"

"I don't know."

She folded her arms.

"I think I get the picture, so I'll skip the other questions," she said. "You've got amnesia, yeah?"

"Yes."

"Bloody brilliant."

"Have you?" I asked.

She shook her head.

"No. My name's Karen Swainey, I live in Moorlands Road, Candleford, Hampshire, Great Britain, planet

Earth, with my husband Paul and half a dozen Chihuahuas. I work in the accounts department for a hand and power tools wholesaler. I woke up here about three hours ago, I think, I'm just guessing, and I have no idea how I got here."

I felt a sudden flash of envy. This other version of me had memories, had a biography, had a life she could remember. I had nothing. The envy passed in a heartbeat and was replaced by something that could only have been dread as I realized that, given all the facts at her disposal versus the nothing that I had, she had a more legitimate claim to being real than I did… the case for myself and all these corpses being versions of her, rather than versions of me, was undeniably stronger than my own claim.

She was looking at me with a level gaze.

"Yeah," she said, but not unkindly. "I'm only guessing, but I think I know what you're thinking. And yeah, I think that too."

I was breathing heavily. The dread was morphing into panic, existential horror mounting within me. I staggered, almost fell, but then she was there holding me up.

"Calm down," she said. "It's okay. I'm frightened too."

"You don't seem to be."

"I'm good at keeping my head. I'm one of those people who thrive in a crisis… although this," she gestured around us, "is stretching things a bit."

I stood up under my own power again.

"Thank you," I said.

She shrugged, and then frowned, thinking.

"You called this a train, didn't you?" she said.

"Yes. The word seemed to fit."

She was looking around and nodding.

"I see where you're coming from. It is like a train carriage, or the inside of an airplane, only really basic, more like the idea of a train hastily scribbled on the back of an envelope."

The surprise must have been evident on my face, because when she looked back at me she asked me what I was goggling at.

"The way you described our situation," I said, "the train as an idea of a train written down in haste, not fully fleshed out. That's exactly right. You've captured the essence of our surroundings perfectly, in just one sentence."

"Thanks, I suppose," she said uncertainly. "I wanted to be a writer when I was younger, before life and other shit happened."

"Do you have any other thoughts?"

She blew out her cheeks, looking down at the corpse that had been sitting beside her. It was a version of me of about fifty years of age, laughter lines spraying from the corners of its eyes, long, greying hair tied back into a bun with a strip of leather. There was a neat, puckered hole in the center of its forehead, a trail of dried blood running down from it, flowing down the left side of its nose, then over its closed lips, onto his chin where it had clotted in a thin strip of beard.

"You came from that direction?" she said, pointing back down the train.

"Yes."

"Far?"

"I don't know. There's no way of determining distance."

She looked around us again.

"Actually, I think there is," she said,

V
MILE

SHE was staring into the abyss, and perhaps the abyss was staring into her.

"I don't know what's more disturbing; the bodies, or the fact there's nothing out there."

She had stopped to gaze out of window four hundred and forty.

We had travelled one mile.

Karen's way of estimating how far we had travelled was so obvious I should have figured it out for myself. The windows were uniformly the same length; all we had to do estimate that length, then multiply that by the number we passed, adjusting for the gap of one set of seats between them.

The windows we put at nine-foot-long, with the gap being three feet. Total, twelve feet. There are five thousand two hundred and eighty feet in a mile, so when we reached window number four hundred and forty we had travelled our first mile together.

I had no idea of the distance I had covered before I had met Karen.

"It's not dark," she said, speaking mainly to herself. "That's not it. It's not just a lack of light... it's a lack of anything."

At Karen's insistence, we had tried to break a window and found the glass material far stronger than our punches and kicks. This was just as well, I supposed, as if there truly was an empty void outside the train, what was the point? We wouldn't be going anywhere, or at least, plummeting into nothingness was as much of a straight line as our current course of travelling up the length of the train.

She shuddered as if she had shared my thought of a fall into eternal darkness.

"We should get going," she said.

"Why?" I asked.

She looked puzzled.

"What do you mean, why?"

"You said that we should get going," I said. "And while I will continue with you on our current course, I'd like to know why you think we *should*."

"That's just... weird."

"I don't think so. I've been walking simply to sate my curiosity, but what you said implied purpose and urgency."

She was staring at me.

I stared back.

"Let's just go," she said.

We counted off the miles and Karen talked. She told me all about her life; about her husband, how they had met at work and fallen for one another despite a generation gap between them; about her pet

Chihuahuas, which turned out to be a breed of dog, who had bizarre names like Squirrel-Ass and Seasick; about the holiday of a lifetime her and her husband were planning to a place called Bermuda for his sixtieth birthday... she talked non-stop, whilst I held up my end of the one-sided conversation with inane single syllable comments or wordless vocalizations of surprise or interest or wonder.

I suspected she was talking so much as a nervous reaction to our strange situation. I wondered at my own calm, but then reached the logical assumption that, having no personal memories, I had nothing to compare it to, and without that contrast my emotional reaction had nowhere to go. Because of my blank memory, the seemingly endless proto-train filled with corpses was all I had ever known. I had no other experiences to rank it against and so form a response. This was why I had asked Karen "why" when she used the word "should". I genuinely wanted to know what her rationale was.

As she talked and we walked, occasionally stepping over corpses, I examined the other versions of us -I addressed my own existential disquiet by use of the plural, making both Karen and myself equal- and tried to catalogue what I could. More variations were appearing, including missing limbs, extra appendages, or misplaced organs; young and old and fat and thin, there were now also variations on these who were quadriplegics, or who had a dozen fingers on each hand, or had pairs of noses growing where there should have been eye sockets. These differences seemed to be genetic rather than occasioned by environment, as other disfigurements like strawberry birthmarks and cleft palates were also in evidence.

Karen stopped, both walking and talking, and turned to me.

"You don't have a name, do you?" she asked.

"I don't know," I said. "I would guess that I do, but I don't recall it owing to my lack of memory, so for all intents and purposes I am currently anonymous."

"And you take forever to say almost nothing," she said. "You need a name." She pursed her lips, thinking. "How about Gavin?"

"I don't like that name."

"Why not?"

"I just don't," I said. The truth was I was a little stung by her comment about how it took me forever to say almost nothing. I took being stung as yet more evidence that I was not a robot.

"Whiney sod, aren't you?" said Karen. "It's a perfectly good name."

"Why Gavin?"

"Because I think you look like a Gavin."

"Oh really?" I said. "And what does a Gavin look like?"

"Like a whiney sod," she said, and then grinned. "Yeah! Gavin Whiney! That'll do until you remember who you are."

"I'm not sure I care for that name," I said.

"Can you think of a better one?"

I thought about it for a while.

"I can't," I admitted.

"So, no objection then?"

"Yes, I object."

She sighed.

"Why?"

"Because," I said, "you told me all your dog's names. You said their names were Soupy, Skeet, Soo-Z, Squirrel-Ass, and Seasick."

"Fuck me, a bloke who listens when a woman talks. Yeah, those are my babies' names, so what?"

"I think that proves you aren't very good at names."

"Alright then, have another crack at it; can you think of a better one?"

I thought about it for a while.

"I still can't," I admitted.

She smirked.

"Fine, Gavin Whiney it is. C'mon Gav, let's push on, shall we?"

And so, we pushed on.

VI
MELTDOWN

"AN El Salvadoran Gavin, a Canadian Gavin, a Polish Gavin…"

I still didn't like the name Gavin and Karen knew it, so when the other versions of us began to have distinctly different skin tones and other ethnically diverse genetic traits, she needled me by naming each Gavin and assigning them a country of origin.

"…a Laotian Gavin, a New Zealander Gavin, a Somalian Gavin…"

These countries were unknown to me. I was aware that my species was divided up into many diverse races, and so wasn't surprised when the corpses began to display such differences as darker skin tones, but geopolitics was out of my sphere of knowledge.

"…an Argentinian Gavin, a Jamaican Gavin, a North Korean Gavin…"

I had no idea whether Karen's assignation of nationality to the corpses she pointed to at random was correct, so I couldn't contradict her and end her litany of Gavin, Gavin, Gavin…

"…a Gavin from Vatican City!" she declared. "A Gavin from Lesotho! A Gavin from San Marino! And what do all *these* Gavin's have in common?"

She stopped walking and spun in the aisle to face me.

"They're all dead," I ventured.

"Wrong! Those last three Gavin's each came from a country that shares a border with only one other country, and has no coastline! I am queen of the pub quiz trivia round, geography a specialty!"

Her eyes were wide and her pupils were dilated. She was breathing long, deep breaths.

At some point during the past five miles -two thousand two hundred windows and counting- her mind had broken.

"You appear to be in a deal of mental distress," I said.

She just stared at me.

"Would it help if we talked about whatever is distressing you?"

She blinked.

"You're…" she said slowly. "You are… what are you? You're truly something. Yeah, that's what you are. Yes, I am in mental distress. Well done. Well observed. I'd have put it another way, like, saying that I'm losing my fucking mind, but yeah, you got the gist of it."

She sat down suddenly, as if she had been pushed backwards. She dropped into the lap of a black version of us with three lip piercings, his head clean shaven and a tattoo of a brain drawn upon his scalp, as if the top of his skull had been cleanly removed.

Karen looked at him, then looked at me.

"And now I'm a ventriloquist's dummy," she said. She stiffened her whole body; when she spoke again she made her mouth flap open and closed without shaping her words, and her eyes rocked back and forth. "Gottle of gear, gottle of gear!"

She started laughing, but it wasn't laughter with joy as its engine. Fear powered this laughter, high and jagged. She laughed and she laughed until the sound was indistinguishable from screaming.

I reached forward and gripped her face, fingers and thumb gripping her cheeks, not quite clamping over her mouth but close. I didn't know precisely what I planned to do, but I decided that I wanted her to stop, and when my fingers touched her face she did, suddenly, her eyes terrified.

"What's going on?" she asked, her mouth caught in the pincer of my hand.

"You know what's going on," I answered. "You and I are aboard something that resembles a train, filled with dead versions of ourselves. Nothing more and nothing less. I am guessing the cumulative weight of the experience has caused a fracture in your mental state, perhaps disabling any coping mechanism you had been using until this point."

I let go of her face.

She closed her eyes.

"I told you I wanted to be a writer?" she asked, and continued without hearing my answer. "That's because I love reading. I'll read almost anything, but I like wild sci-fi best, the crazier the better. And I've just been going over and over all the stupid, worn out cliché's in my head; this is a dream, a hallucination, a coma fantasy, a computer simulation. That this isn't real, y'know?"

She started sobbing, her eyes still closed.

"But it is real," she said, and her hands covered her face. "It just hit me suddenly. This is insane and it's *real.*"

I didn't know what to say. The reality of the situation was self-evident to me, but then again, I had nothing to compare it to, no memory of things being other than they were to point to and suggest one experience had more validity than the other.

Eventually her sobbing dissipated. Her hands fell away from her face and she opened red-rimmed eyes to look at me, then look at the corpse in whose lap she sat.

"Why am I the only one?" she asked.

"You're not," I said. "There's thousands of us. You and me and all the corpses."

"No!" she snapped, standing up and brushing at the seat of her trousers. "I mean, why am I the only female?"

I thought about this. I looked around, confirming if nothing else that there weren't any female corpses of us in the immediate area.

"Are you sure you're the only one?" I asked.

"Have you seen any other tits?"

I looked at her chest. If there had been any others, certainly any as large as hers, then the answer was no.

I told her this.

"That would tend to suggest that I'm the only one then, doesn't it? So why? Why, when there are versions of us that are so different, so many different 'usses', dwarf usses, and Native-American usses, and uses with our hair done up in four-foot-tall blue beehives, why am I the only female?"

"I don't know," I said.

"How did I know you were going to say that?"

"That is something else I don't know."

"It was a rhetorical question."

"Oh."

She sighed.

"Let's go," she said. "I think that little meltdown ought to tide me over for a few miles. How far have we gone now?"

I told her the window count and what that amounted to in miles.

She sighed again.

VII
RISING

WE walked through a mile length of the train which was full of disemboweled versions of us whose lengths of small and large intestines had been wound around and about and up and over the seats and bodies into a crisscrossing web. We had to step gingerly over lengths of taut gut at ankle height and slip under bloody-slippery lengths that were wrapped around throats and back and forth across the width of the train.

We walked through a section of the train in which the corpses seemed to all be identical to me, with not even the minor cosmetic differences I had noticed at the very start of the journey, before I met Karen. These corpses seemed so identical, and were so remarkable for this fact -as I was not particularly remarkable in any way- that we spent some time pulling dead copies of me out of their seats to examine them more carefully, only to discover that it was only in the smallest and almost unnoticeable ways that each was still uniquely different. One had a tattoo of a smiley yellow face -an *emoji*, Karen called it- tattooed on the pad of the big toe on his right foot; another had a pale half-moon scar just above his hairline on his forehead, a healed wound from stitches sutured in early childhood; whilst others still only differed in the placement of a mole next to their navel, varying in distance from an inch to three inches.

We found a version of us whose immensely long beard had been plaited into a noose, with which he had been hung to death.

We found a version of us with a parasitic twin growing from the side of its neck; in turn this parasitic miniature version of us also had a twin growing from its neck, and that twin also did, which in turn also did, and so on until the outgrowths of parasitic twins sporting their own parasitic versions grew too small to see.

We found versions of us which were teratologically fabulous, and versions of us which were utterly banal. Usses with keyhole-shaped eye sockets. Usses with fingers which were miniature arms ending in miniature hands. Usses that had no body hair, but instead sported the fleshy growths of chickens; no beards, but rather wattles, and no hair, but coxcombs instead.

After twenty-six miles of bizarre and atrocious sights, Karen said, "I'm hungry."

I realized that I was hungry too.

"But there's nothing to eat," I pointed out.

"No," she said. "No, there's not, you're right."

"So where does that leave us?"

We'd stopped in a section of the train where all the usses had incredibly long necks. Those corpses that were still seated had necks so long their heads brushed the ceiling, so that slack, dead faces loomed over us. The cause of death for most of these bodies seemed to have been execution at point blank range with various guns; bullet holes in faces dripped thick blood down on us.

"Well," said Karen, "if I can quote you, 'I don't know.' Unless this train has a buffet car and we haven't reached it yet. But that seems highly un-fucking-likely."

"We could eat one of the bodies," I said.

Karen's expression when I suggested this was complicated. By the twists of her mouth and her eyebrows it seemed to want to convey that she was shocked at the idea, with an afterglow of disgust at the fact that I would even suggest it, but underlying this was something in her eyes that said that he had already had the thought and had quietly stored it away for later perusal.

"Cannibalism? Are you joking?"

"No, just being logical. There's nothing else to eat and we have yet to come across any evidence that our situation is going to radically change in the immediate future. You expressed the idea yourself when you mooted the un-fucking-likely existence of a buffet car... if I can quote you."

"Don't be a smart arse," she said. "And I'm not eating any dead bodies until... no, fuck it, I'm not going to say it! We must come across something different eventually! Because if this was a computer simulation we were in, or whatever, there would have to be some sort of point to it, which means something has to happen, we have to find food or something."

There was something I'd been thinking about for the past two miles which I decided to mention now.

"I think something has started to happen," I said.

Karen cocked her head slightly.

"What are you on about?"

"At first, I thought there was something wrong with my perceptions," I said. "But I've slowly grown more and more certain about it."

"What?"

"We're not on a flat surface anymore," I said. "We're on an incline. We're very slowly climbing up a slope."

Karen looked both surprised and angry.

"Are you taking the piss? How could we be going up a slope? It doesn't feel like we're climbing up a slope."

"That's because it's so gentle. It started about five miles back. Look."

I pointed back the way we came, and then pointed forward.

Karen followed my finger. At first, she frowned, but then she looked back and forth again, and again, double and triple checking what she saw.

"You're right, the vanishing point is higher going forward!" she said.

"Therefore, we must be walking up an incline."

"Then let's keep going!"

My revelation about the change in our surroundings had dispelled all talk of hunger and flesh eating, at least for the time being, and so we kept going. Karen was walking a little more quickly, a lot more determinedly, her hips swinging wider, her huge round buttocks pumping up and down, and I felt a sudden erotic thrill which was just as quickly chilled by an odd sort of disgust. I had just felt a burst of lust towards what was basically myself; was that perverse? Was it wrong? She could have been my twin, which would have made such a thought incestuous. But I knew that she wasn't a blood relative of mine. On some level that we had both taken for granted, we knew we were the same person.

Maybe it was perverse. Maybe there was something more wrong with me than amnesia; after all, I had been the one to propose eating one of our other selves.

VIII
CLIMB

WE were half a mile up when we decided to make camp, mainly because of the hollow chocolate us which turned out to be full of jelly beans.

We had walked for nearly a dozen miles before the incline we were on became truly noticeable. During that time, we hadn't spoken, as Karen was still marching determinedly and I was trying to distract myself from my almost-incest thoughts by counting the windows and scanning the corpses we were swiftly passing.

Increasingly truly bizarre versions of us were appearing in the ranks of the dead. The variations and combinations of cosmetic, minor, and major differences continued to produce a seemingly infinite variety of possible other usses, but increasingly I noticed corpses which could only be described as unique… though as soon as I had noticed them whatever property had cast them as radically different from every other corpse was added to the general pool of variations in upcoming ranks. For example; in a window seat on our right, window seven thousand three hundred and seventeen to be exact, there was a version of us which was a wooden marionette puppet. It looked precisely like me, my height, my beard, everything, save that its features and its clothes were painted on to its crudely made body, and its cause of death was a catastrophic gash in the side of its head, perhaps caused by an axe or a shovel. This gash was filled with painted wooden brains.

Two hundred and forty-two windows later, I saw another puppet us, except this one had no beard, only a toothbrush moustache. It had also been killed differently, bisected at the waist, so that its legs were lying on the ground and the torso sat upon the seat.

This made me wonder if there was a pattern, or at least a set of rules that governed our environment. Was the train entire, or was it being created as we moved, somehow brought into existence just beyond the vanishing point ahead, freshly created seats being stocked with corpses, receding as we approached.

It was a possibility, but there was no evidence.

And besides, what did that mean for the fact that the nature of the train was changing? Incrementally, slowly, the slope was getting steeper. Eventually we found ourselves having to walk up an incline as steep as a set of stairs, using the backs of the seats as handrails.

After a quarter mile of this Karen suddenly stopped and looked back at me.

"Gav, step to one side, would you?"

Then she grabbed the corpse sat in the seat to her left and hauled it into the aisle. When she let go it went tumbling past me, skidding back down the length of the train until it reached the vanishing point far, far below us.

Karen had flopped back in the seat.

"I take my babies out for two, sometimes three walks a day," she said breathlessly. "I mean, that keeps me pretty fit, but this is… it's like climbing a mountain or something."

I pulled the corpse from the seat across the aisle and sent it flailing away so I could have its seat.

"I suppose I'm tired too," I said.

Karen laughed.

"Look, being sat like this, tilted back, it's like being on a roller coaster," she said. "Y'know, when its slowly dragging you to the top of a rise."

I tried to picture a roller coaster. I couldn't, or at least, not a particular one. I knew what she meant, and I could even envision the rough form of such things, but as with everything else, I only knew it as a concept.

I looked at the corpse I was sat next to. This version of us was an albino with antlers. There was a dried foam of blood on his lips. He'd been poisoned.

"Paul can't go on roller coasters," said Karen. "He has a bad heart. He has an IUD for it, y'know, like a pacemaker only a lot more high-tech. It's incredible really, it not only regulates his heartbeats but it makes a record of everything it's done during the day, what his heart rate was like and if it had to give him a little jolt to get back in rhythm, and at night it wirelessly downloads the data into this device on his bedside table, whilst we're asleep. Isn't that amazing, they talk to each other, the little machine in his chest and the one next to our bed? Then that device sends the data to the hospital so they can keep an eye out for any irregularities, and if they think he needs a check-up they just call us in." She was crying. "I wish I was next to him now, dreaming this whilst the little machines talk to each other in the dark."

I had no notion of what I could or should say, so I kept quiet. I kept quiet whilst Karen sobbed and it seemed a long time before she stopped. I only dared to look at her when I heard her getting out of the seat.

"Right, I've had my cloudburst," she said. "Let's go, there's bound to be something to eat on this fucking train, somewhere."

I would have questioned the wisdom of this, but then realized that would be futile, and would only make my companion angry. But as it turned out, it wasn't long after the floor became fully vertical and we were forced to use the seats as ladder rungs to climb up, that we found a version of us who was made of food.

IX
UNIVERSES

KAREN had eaten his entire head on her own, whilst I had only managed his hands.

Even as we climbed I had kept count of the windows, which was how I knew we were half a mile up. The seats were still full of corpses, although now they could be said to not be sat so much as lying in the seats, and each of us had taken a side, left and right, to climb up ladder-style. It was Karen who had come across the corpse of a food version of us.

We threw the other bodies out of their seats, sent them tumbling down the long chimney the train had become, and they rapidly become dots, specks, gone beyond the vanishing point. The twin seats on either side of the train that they had occupied became little cells for us, though precarious, as the backs of the seats opened onto the half-mile fall back down the train's length. We sat on the backs of the aisle seats, legs dangling over the edge, whilst Karen dismembered the corpse.

"Doesn't this still count as cannibalism?" I asked.

"I don't care," said Karen, most of her lower face covered in chocolate.

I had finished the hands whilst she was still chewing forehead.

"I've had a thought," she said, mouth full of chocolate. "A sort of a vague inkling about what's happening to us."

"A vague inkling is more than I have," I said. "Please, go on. Explain."

"It's to do with the multiverse," she said.

The word was a concept I was not familiar with. I said so.

She had finished eating, and loosened the button on her trousers to accommodate a swollen belly.

"Fuck me, I needed that," she sighed. "You don't know what the multiverse is?"

Her unbuttoning her trousers and then saying "fuck me" momentarily disoriented me, causing the mixed feelings of lust and disgust to surface again. I rallied quickly, hoping she wouldn't notice my hesitation.

"Multiverse? No. The word isn't known to me."

There were still substantial chunks of the chocolate corpse in her cell with her, which she carefully pushed towards the window. As she did so I couldn't help noticing the swell of her stomach, and a few curls of pubic hair caught between that curve of flesh and the hem of her simple lacey underwear.

"We'd better save everything we can, there's no telling when we'll come across another food us," she said. "Right. The multiverse. Well, it's a science-fiction concept that says there's more than one universe, there is an infinite number, and they're all different. Some are different, and some are almost identical. Like, there could be… no," she shook her head, "there is, there must be, a universe where people are made from food, and in that universe the version of us was our friend here. But in another universe, there's a version of us who is the same as you, only he had three more hairs on his head then you do. Because with an infinite number of universes, all universes must happen. Do you understand?"

"I think so."

"The way I understand it, every time a decision is made, a universe splits in two," she said. "So, in one universe you have the decision going one way, and in the other things play out with the other decision having happened. I mean, every time an outcome can change, starting from right after the Big Bang, the universe divided like cells replicating, and each new universe was different to reflect the opposing outcomes. Obviously, there weren't people making decisions, but there were quantum states in which things could turn out one way or the other, which is how you end up with some really weird universes. But also, when people make choices; like, if you must make a choice between having sugar in your coffee or not, then the universe will split into two universes, one where you did have sugar and one where you didn't. Are you still following me?"

"Yes," I said; and I hadn't only been following what she said, but had begun to explore it on my own. "That's a very disturbing concept."

She looked puzzled.

"Why?" she asked.

I attempted to put into words some of my own mental exploration of what I understood.

"We are surrounded by dead bodies, which I guess has colored my thinking," I said. "But if I understand this multiverse concept, does that mean every time someone thinks about killing someone there is suddenly a universe where they did, and another where they didn't?"

"Yeah…" said Karen, looking uncertain.

"Then in the universe where they did kill someone, they might kill again?"

Karen said nothing.

"And then again. And again. Because all the universes must happen. So, that means there's a universe where you or I or whatever we are has killed everyone and everything."

Karen's eyes had widened until I could see the white all the way around her irises.

"What the fuck?" she said. "I've never… I've never thought of it like that, but you're right. There are universes where I've killed Paul, and all my babies, and my mum and… oh my God…"

Karen turned her head to one side and vomited over the back of the seat she was sat on. A glutinous mix of melted chocolate and stomach acid fell in a twisting, splattering rope down and down and out of sight.

"Are you okay?" I asked.

Karen was gagging, but still managed to look up and murder me with a glare.

I could forgive that look. It was an asinine question to ask someone in obvious distress.

"Sorry," I said.

She spat.

"It's fine," she said. "It's just that I thought about,

y'know, what I just said, and suddenly my heart was racing and I was all panicky. God, I don't even want to think about... No, I won't."

She shuddered.

I decided to try being constructive.

"Perhaps we should stay here for some time and rest," I said. "We've both been moving for many miles and we probably need to rejuvenate. And you'll need to eat again."

Karen nodded, her face white and greasy looking from nausea.

"Not a bad plan," she said. "I think maybe I could go for a kip. But one of us needs to stay awake. We're in a bit of a precarious position; wouldn't be good to go rolling over in our sleep."

She was referring to the drop.

"I don't think that will be a problem," I said. "I have an idea."

I unbuttoned my blue shirt and pulled it off. Then I tied one arm to the bolted down leg of the window seat in front of me or overhead, depending on perspective, and tied the other arm around my right wrist. My arm was securely fastened, anchoring me to the seat above/ in front of me.

Karen snorted.

"Well, as long as we don't pull on them too hard the stitching should hold," she said, and followed my lead, moving chunks of chocolate corpse around to make room for herself.

With a vague sense of security, we each lay down in our respective cell, and though I couldn't speak for Karen, I was asleep in moments.

X
INCEST

I woke up to find my or our or her lips engulfing the head of my penis and my or our or her vagina gaping above my mouth.

Karen had abandoned her seats and climbed across the aisle to me. I must have been in a deep sleep for her to have not only shed her clothes, but also positioned herself into the sixty-nine positions without awakening me, but the sudden sensation of full, moist lips sucking my engorged glans into her mouth had woken me up.

"Karen? What…" was all I had time to say before the vagina that I would have had if I were female was thrust into my face. It was hot and extremely wet and it smelled spicy.

I felt lips slide off the end of my penis, though two hands still gripped it hard around the root, squeezing it so that the blood bloated out the veins.

"Eat my cunt," she snarled, and then plunged down onto me again.

I could feel the weight of her breasts resting on my stomach, her hands gripping my thighs for support. She hadn't pinned my arms though, allowing me to reach around and grab the cheeks of her rear. The sheer pleasure radiating from my groin eliminated conscious thought and left only raw instinct, so I pulled her down onto my mouth and began sucking and licking and guzzling at her, lapping up the hot juice that overflowed and dripped down my chin.

My enthusiasm was matched by her, her mouth swallowing more and more of me even as her grip tightened and pumped.

We became one single creature, a complete whole, perfect and complete unto itself, knowing nothing and caring for even less beyond our combined nervous system of wet-electrified membranes fused at either orifice into a feedback loop of escalating pleasure and tightening muscle. No words, only noises, organic machine noises as throbbing meat pistoned inside lubricated tightness, sighs like steam escaping, diaphragm deep moans, sticky noises, wet noises, sounds of suction.

I don't know who orgasmed first. We may have come together. It was hard to tell because of the amount of sexual fluids that had been gushing from her almost the entire time; maybe she had been coming over and over again and was only satiated when I had finally exploded deep in her throat, my inarticulate bellow of ecstasy roared against her overheated sex, pulsing and pulsing within the stricture of her teeth almost clamped shut around my shaft, then an ebbing away, tide receding. After we were done Karen collapsed next to me, almost pushing me to the edge. Her whole body was slick with sweat, long strands of black hair plastered to her forehead and cheeks.

"I don't…" she gasped. "I…"

"That was interesting," I said.

"I don't know what happened," said Karen. "I woke up and I was feeling lonely and scared, so I thought I'd see if you wouldn't mind cuddling… but then I saw you had a hardon, you had this massive bulge in your trousers, and you were asleep and I wanted to know what it would… I wanted to know what my cock would look like, if I had one."

The organ in question was deflated and drying stickily. I stuffed it back into my trousers, Karen watching.

"Well, you found out."

"I couldn't stop myself!" she said. "I just got so turned on! And y'know what? I was disgusted too, because even though I wanted to, and then we did, it felt wrong. It felt like I was fucking my brother, or my dad, or something."

Then she was awkwardly clambering out of my cell, climbing back across the aisle, throwing her clothes ahead of her. When she was back in her own seats she started to dress herself again in the confined space, at the same time avoiding my gaze.

I considered what she said.

"I confess, I've had thoughts about you," I told her. "Lust thoughts, at times. I understand what you mean. They felt incestuous."

Karen sobbed.

"Incestuous… God that's such an ugly word," she said. "I'm disgusting. We're disgusting."

She picked up a chocolate foot and had eaten the

toes off it before she frowned, snarled, and threw it at me. It struck my chest and broke, spilling jelly beans.

"Stop looking at me!" she screamed. "Don't you look at me like that!"

I said nothing for a few moments. She had curled her legs up and bowed her head.

"You do realize," I said at last, "that strictly speaking, no matter what our feelings on the matter, the absolute worst thing you could have called that experience was masturbation?"

Two moments passed, and then she looked up.

"If you and I are the same person," I said, "from different multiverses, if we accept that premise, then essentially what we just did was only... self-love." I searched for a better word. "A wank. That was just a wank."

She was considering my words.

"I think you might be right," she said slowly. "Yeah, masturbating. Your mouth, my mouth. Y'know, we were watching TV one night, me and Paul, with all the babies on the sofa, and Squirrel-Arse started licking his balls, and Paul said, 'I wish I could do that', and I said, 'Give him a biscuit and he might let you.'"

She laughed.

"I got to do the one thing no-one has ever done!" she said. "I got to go and fuck myself!"

XI
CEILING

WALKING across a ceiling covered in corpses was hard going.

After we had recovered from our mutual masturbation we ate some more of the chocolate corpse, sharing out its jelly bean blood and discovering that its internal organs were all as delicious as its flesh; it had a liver of gingerbread, marzipan kidneys, and a heart made of red licorice. Thus, rested and feasted, we began our climb again, once more using the ranks of seats as crude ladders, climbing past more seated corpses of increasing weirdness.

I couldn't catalogue the bizarreries in the same studious fashion as I had at the beginning of our journey, as climbing required concentration. Aware that we had a half mile drop back down the aisle below us, we grew increasingly cautious as that distance expanded. Still, the most notable new variations continued to catch my eye, despite the increasing peril of our situation.

The species boundary was crossed. There were reptilian usses, scaled and tailed versions who Karen surmised we would have been if dinosaurs had survived and evolved into bipeds instead of birds. There were upright dog versions of us, which delighted Karen; she called them strange words like Alsatian, Labradoodle, Chinese Crested, Pug. I was startled when we saw a version of us that was clearly some grotesque mutation of the centipede family, though it set Karen off on a journey of speculation as to what sort of a world it could have come from.

I observed how talkative Karen had become, particularly when we should perhaps have been conserving our energy for the climb.

"I always get chatty after a fuck," she told me. "Paul just rolls on his side, farts, and nods off, so I end up talking to my babies. It's actually a bit weird having an audience who knows what I'm saying. Anyway, if we need to stop for another rest we'll just do the same as before, bed down on the backs of some of these seats."

"That is becoming increasingly unlikely," I said.

"Eh? What do you mean?"

"Our angle of ascent has increased," I said, and decided to demonstrate by letting my feet dangle. When I did so, gripping on extra tight with my hands, I let Karen have a moment to digest what she was seeing, something I had intuited.

"Oh shit, you're right! It's curving!"

If the climb had still been truly vertical, my dangling body would have been exactly parallel to the backs of the seats, but it was not. My feet were closer to the ceiling than my head. The body of the train was curling over backwards.

"We're going to need to move more slowly as we climb," I said. "Until the ceiling is level enough to jump down onto. We will have to hang upside down for a while."

"No worries, just like the monkey bars in a kiddies' playground."

We continued, and Karen grew quiet. The going became much harder, as we could rely on our feet less and less to support our weight, going gradually from climbing to hanging, our feet not supporting us at all, but bracing us, as we crawled or swung as much as climbed. This could not go on for long, as neither of us was well developed in the muscles of our arms and chests, and so we both kept glancing down towards the ceiling, attempting to judge when the angle was not so steep that, should we allow ourselves to drop, we shouldn't immediately begin sliding down back the way we came.

In the end, it was the corpses that told us when it would be safe to fall onto the ceiling and continue our ascent on foot.

At some point neither of us noticed -our attention having become fully involved in the strenuous exercise of crawling/swinging/climbing on a steepening curve- the seats had been vacated of corpses. Logically, the seats had become so inverted that corpses could simply not have remained in them, even if it were possible to force them into upside down seating positions. But, not a moment too soon for our flagging strength and aching arm muscles, there were corpses piled on the ceiling, as if they had been seated previously, and had tumbled out when the train had become inverted. The fact that these bodies had not slid back down the slope indicated that it was sufficiently steep for us to drop down onto, and so we did.

The corpses cushioned us, and even though the ceiling was closer to horizontal than vertical it was still as steep as a flight of stairs and we both scrambled to upright ourselves for fear of tumbling back down the way we had so painstakingly progressed.

"Are you alright?" Karen asked me.

"I am," I said.

There was a period of quiet. Karen only gazed at me.

"What?" I asked.

"Y'know, the normal thing would be for you to ask me if I was alright as well," she said.

"Okay," I said. "I believe I understand the social convention at work, a reciprocal if empty gesture of concern for one another's physical well-being," I told her. "Are you alright?"

She threw her hands up.

"I don't believe you!" she said, turned, and began to climb over the corpses that littered the ceiling, heading further up the train.

I wasn't sure what to make of her behavior, but rather then remain behind to puzzle it out I decided to continue following her on our journey up the train.

The going was difficult. The reason the going was difficult was owing to three separate factors; first, we were both exhausted from our progress so far. Our ascent had been long and arduous, particularly in the last portion where we had been hanging as much as climbing. Second, the ceiling was still at a steep angle, so it was still a lot like walking up stairs. And finally, the corpses covered the ceiling so thickly that they were like a matt of flesh, arms and legs tangled together, so that we had to walk across them, which was both unpleasant and treacherous, as flesh and blood are an unsteady surface at best.

XII
NAMES

FOR the past mile, the corpses had all been decapitated. I thought about telling Karen, but decided not to. What would have been the point?

The ceiling had levelled out enough that we felt comfortable stopping at the first corpse of a food us that we came upon. This version of us seemed to be made of fruit and vegetables.

"It's like something out of an Arcimboldo painting," she said.

"What's that?" I asked.

"You don't know what a painting is?"

I thought.

"Yes," I said. "I know what a painting is. I don't know what an Arcimboldo painting is."

"Arcimboldo was an artist," Karen said. "From donkey's years ago. He did these really cool pictures of people made from things, like a portrait of a librarian who was made from books. He did a load of them where people were made from food, y'know, like having a beard of carrots, or a nose that was a pear. This us looks like he could have stepped out of an Arcimboldo painting."

She had settled herself cross-legged on the chest of a version of us who had vibrant blue skin and puffy white hair. He had huge white eyebrows and a big white beard and a massive white Afro haircut. He had tattoos across his left cheek in the shapes of small black V shapes, and he wore earrings, one of a cartoon smiling sun and the other of a cartoon scowling moon. I was sat next to her, on the same corpse's thighs.

Karen was cradling the fruit and vegetable version of us in her lap.

"God I'm thirsty," she said. "How about you?"

I was as well. I told her so.

"I have an idea…"

She leant her head down and bit into our neck, biting through banana skin. She clamped her mouth down and began to suck. After a while she released her suction hold and gasped, her lips and teeth smeared red.

"Tomato juice for blood!" she said. "Hits the spot!"

She offered me the body and I leant forward to suck on the wound she had made, sucked and drank the delicious juice to slake my thirst. When I was done, Karen was grinning a bloody grin.

"And now a little mutilation," she said.

She pulled off one of our apple cheeks and took a bite. She munched it thoughtfully for a moment, then nodded.

"Hmm," she said. "Hmm, good. Tastes like a Pink Lady. I love Pink Lady's, not like those bloody flavorless Granny Smith's…"

My bewilderment was wrought clearly on my face

for her to see and react to.

"You do know what this is?" she asked, waggling the bitten apple at me.

"Yes," I said. "It's a piece of fruit. An apple."

"Here."

She handed it to me. I took a bite. It was very, very sweet, almost too sweet.

"So, what was it I said that confused you?" Karen asked. "I saw it plain as day on your face, you looked like I was talking Martian."

This also confused me, but I addressed her question rather than raise one of my own.

"The apple, you said it tasted like a Pink Lady. You also said that it wasn't without flavor, like Granny Smith."

"Yeah, so?"

"Well, notwithstanding the chocolate us we ate, and this fruit and vegetable us we are going to eat, you were initially dead set against cannibalism."

She had taken another bite of the apple. She was chewing with only one side of her mouth.

"Yeah," she repeated, through a mouth full of chewed up apple flesh. "So?"

"But by your own admission you've eaten pink women and grandmothers. I don't understand your original objection."

Her chewing slowed, then stopped. Her eyes were narrowed.

She swallowed. Her eyes were still narrowed, suspicious.

"Are you serious?" she asked, then answered her own question. "You are. You're being serious."

Seeing as though she had answered the question correctly, I had nothing to add.

Her head tilted slightly.

"I think…" she said. "I think… you don't really understand proper nouns, do you?"

"A proper noun refers to a unique entity," I said. "Rather than a common noun which refers to a class of entities."

"You answered that like a robot," she said, which sent a chill trickling down my vertebrae. "How about an example?"

"Your name is Karen Swainey," I said. "Your husband's name is Paul. You have five Chihuahua dogs called Soupy, Skeet, Soo-Z, Squirrel-Ass, and Seasick. These are all proper nouns."

She was nodding.

"That's right…" She paused. "But you don't know that Pink Ladies and Granny Smiths are apples."

"No," I said, trying to understand. "You're saying these apples have names?"

"Yeah. No. Sort of. Look, various kinds of apples have different names. Here, you said 'Chihuahua dogs' as if it was all one thing. Describe a dog."

I described a dog. Four legs, covered in fur, known for wagging their tails and barking and burying bones.

"That's just rough sketch," said Karen. "Do you think all dogs are the same? Do you know what a Dalmatian is? Can you describe one? Can you describe a Chihuahua?"

I thought about it. I couldn't. I said so.

"So, you don't know that a Dalmatian is quite a big dog with white fur and black spots, or that a Chihuahua is a very small dog with sticky-up ears?"

"I can't picture either of them," I admitted. "I know

what a dog is, but… you said a rough sketch, and that's what's in my head, a vague dog shape."

Karen was quiet as she thought about this.

"So basically, you have knowledge, but no experience?" she said.

"I think that's right," I said. "That is the simplest way to put it."

"It's like you're unfinished," she said, though the quiet reflection in her voice suggested she was speaking her thoughts aloud rather than seeking to engage me in further discussion. "Almost as if you're a one-dimensional character in a crappy book… Oh, shit! No, please don't let this be some kind of post-postmodern metafictional bollocks!"

She picked up the severed head of the fruit and vegetable us by the roots of its mung bean hair, then stood up.

"We'll eat on the way," she said, her voice stern.

"On the way where?" I asked, also standing.

"Wherever this shit-show is going," she said. "I just remembered one of the wankiest plots in all of genre fiction, the one where the characters realize that they are only characters in a story! That's what's going on here, it must be! Come on, maybe there'll be a plot twist to get us out of this crap."

XIII
AVALANCHE

THE corpse avalanche was an accident.

Karen had been describing some of the stories she had tried and failed to write.

"But I think the most ambitious one was this stupid metafiction," she had said, walking across the ceiling-carpet of bodies, gruesome stepping stones, the half-eaten head of fruit and vegetable us swinging in her hand. "I thought it was so clever at the time. I heard once that every human being on Earth could fit onto the Isle of Wight…"

The ceiling was tilting gradually, no longer flat but descending. It seemed the train was curled over on itself in a vast spiral. I was attempting to listen to Karen whilst at the same time making a rough calculation as to when the angle would be too steep for us to safely keep walking down, and we would need to grab hold of the seats as a makeshift ladder again to continue.

I had stopped to ask her to clarify what metafiction

was. She said they were stories where the boundaries between what was fictional and what was not became blurred, and then told me about people called Max Beerbohm and Enoch Soames. I pretended to understand and then she went back to her own story.

"…so, the Isle of Wight is this tiny island off the south coast of England. England is the country I'm from, right? I told you that? Right. Anyway, the island, I went there once, on a day trip with my mum. Weird place. Anyway, someone had worked out the square footage of the island and then figured out the average size of a human being, and figured out there was just enough room for all seven billion of us to cram on there. So, my idea was that one day the entire population of Earth would suddenly find themselves, completely naked, all on the Isle of Wight, and this alien intelligence would speak to them all at the same time telepathically…"

She paused to pull out a stuffed olive eye and a handful of sweetcorn teeth and popped them in her mouth. She offered me the head. I declined. We walked on, her talking again as the ceiling became steeper and steeper.

"Where was I? Yeah, this voice in everyone's head all at once, in whatever language they speak, says that, as a species, we've been judged as worthless, so we've all got to go, except for two people, a man and a woman, who will be saved for an alien zoo or some stupid shit. And the reason we've all been brought together in one place is so we can decide who the lucky two will be, in whatever way we choose… by voting, or a lottery… or a violent bloodbath. Naturally, being humans, things get nasty, and millions of people begin to murder each other."

I didn't say anything. This made her stop walking and look at me. By this point we were moving much more slowly, as the gradient was approaching stair steepness. She stood with one foot planted at an angle, as did I, to keep our balance.

It was a good place to stop. Only half a dozen window lengths in front of us the ceiling was clear of corpses, indicating that the pull of gravity had won out at that point, causing any corpses that had fallen from above to tumble down the length of the train forward and downward. Here was where we needed to jump up and gain a grip on the seats again, and begin the arm-aching task of shinning along whilst hanging upside down until the train's length was vertical enough for us to use the seats as ladders once more, and climb down, or forwards, depending on how you thought of it.

"Well?" said Karen.

"Well what?" I asked.

"Don't you see? Think about it, look at all the parallels! Countless corpses, just two of us alive, man and woman! It's so much like my story idea it can't be a coincidence!"

I thought this over.

"Did you actually write this story?" I asked.

Karen blinked.

"Well," she said, "I had a few goes at it. I mean, I tried to, I wrote a few chapters…"

"You didn't finish it?"

"No," she said. "It's just that… I always start strong, I always have these great ideas for characters and plot twists in my head but I never seem to… I just get frustrated, and then I'll get another great idea and I put whatever I wrote to one side to start on the next thing, and I always tell myself I'll get back to it when…"

She trailed off.

"If you ever wrote the story, then the parallels between it and what we are going through are all in your head," I said. "And they weren't very strong to start with."

"But that's what you don't understand!" she said, almost pleading. "I had the big plot twist in my head, all ready to blow the reader's mind right at the end, it's just that I never got there! And the twist…"

The corpse she had one foot perched on suddenly burst. It was a balloon version of us. Karen shrieked and tottered backwards. The gradient of the ceiling had become so steep that maintaining her balance was impossible, and she fell backwards onto the carpet of corpses.

Apparently, we were stood almost exactly at a balanced point, almost exactly at the point that the steepness became more vertical than horizontal, because her fall dislodged the tangled matt of bodies in such a way that they all began sliding forwards, forwards and inevitably downwards.

Karen screamed again as the tide of corpses she was being swept along with began to speed up, making it impossible for her to gain her feet. I felt the bloated corpse I was stood on beginning that irresistible skid, and I jumped up to grab the backs of the nearest seats above me.

I felt the rigid plastic in my grasp, and for a moment I hung there with the most tenuous grip. Arms and legs laced together in an atrocious jumble, a great mass of the bodies was tumbling down the train with Karen lost amongst them, screaming and screaming.

XIV
DESCENT

I stopped to rest at the point when the backs of the seats were horizontal enough for the corpses to occupy them without sliding out and tumbling down the shaft of the train. The two that were in the seats I intended to spend a few moments resting in were made from glass, hollow glass, filled with contrasting liquids; the one in the aisle seat was full of an effervescent dark caramel colored liquid, whilst the one in the window seat was full of what could only be semen.

Because the train had looped on itself it meant these versions of me weren't lying back as if in the cart of a roller coaster ascending an incline, but were rather sprawled face down against the backs of the seats in front of them, heading down.

I was hanging onto the back of the seats of these bottle versions of me, my feet resting on the backs of the seats in front of theirs. I looked behind me, across the aisle to the opposite two seats. Those corpses were blue-shirted, black trouser wearing versions of me that seemed to be -in the aisle seat- crudely molded out of oily clay, and -in the window seat- an otherwise normal human version of me whose every inch of visible skin was tattooed with the words GUILTY BUT INSANE in multiple unusual sizes, colors, and fonts.

I shoved the bottle man corpses of me up against the window, giving myself just enough room to sit for a few minutes, to catch my breath, and let my trembling arms recover some of their strength.

I allowed myself to lean out and look down the aisle, up the train.

I could just about make out a jumble of still corpses. That had to mark the point where the train ran more horizontal than vertical again. I had only travelled about a fifth of a mile, which compared with the mile up Karen and I had climbed earlier, meant that the train didn't perform a perfect loop.

This was a relief. It meant that Karen had more chance, however slim, of having survived her fall in the avalanche of corpses. It also meant I had less distance to travel before discovering whether that slim chance was no chance or some miracle fluke.

Whilst I waited for my second wind I examined the corpses more closely.

Their flesh truly was glass, or at least seemed so. It was cool and hard to the touch. But it was malleable too, like flesh; I could bend the fingers of their hands, flex their wrists, and turn their heads. Their faces were shaped glass, with shaped glass features. One had a glass beard, and the other had a thin glass moustache. Their eyes were wide open, with irises and pupils etched on. I pulled down their eyelids and saw the glass was frosted, which made sense; if they were the same transparent glass as the rest of the flesh and the hair then they would have had no practical point, because the whole point of eyelids was to shut out the outside world...

The eyelids weren't see through. Which in context made complete sense.

I felt hysteria stir inside me. I wanted to laugh, or scream. Neither. Both.

Because it was funny, that something so insane, even in the midst of the insanity which was my current situation, should make sense. If the eyelids had been transparent it would have been different; but they were frosted, not see-through, and so these corpses had to have come from a lunatic reality where things still made sense. The paradox caused the laughter or the screaming to bubble deep inside me. In what reality could hollow glass versions of me filled with fluid possibly exist? I could not conceive of a universe where the rules of physics and biology were so radically different to those that had seemingly shaped me as flesh and blood, and yet, no matter how alien the underlying mathematical structures of such a universe, had somehow produced copies of myself that could occupy it.

The bizarre notion of a multiverse was suddenly a vast gulf under me, causing my head to swim as a sickening combination of vertigo and déjà vu swept through me, making my very soul feel sick. Existential panic capered close.

I closed my eyes and lowered my head and waited for the soul-nausea to pass.

Gradually it did, and with it faded away the hysteria,

that awful laughter-scream that had been percolating.

I waited until I was certain I was calm. I didn't know how much time passed, but it was renewed urgency that I resolve to climb down and discover what had happened to my female self. I urged myself to not engage in imagining scenarios, but simply to get on with the task of lowering myself quickly but safely down to where the train was level enough that the avalanche had come to a rest.

And as I descended I tried not to think about the smell that floated up to greet me, an odor of opened bodies.

XV
ROBOT

I half hopped, half stumbled down onto the pile of corpses. The sudden unsureness of sundered flesh and broken bones underfoot, in stark contrast to the surety of the hard-plastic seats I had been climbing down, made me feel nauseous. Yes, not long before Karen and I had been walking across a mat of bodies lying on the train's inverted ceiling, but the transition back to such a surface was still unpleasant.

The smell of blood and shit was strong, making the air stickily humid. Many of the corpses had burst open after the long fall, either after their own impact or when subsequent falling bodies had slammed into them. I warily began to descend the pile, trying to pick my way around the worst messes of splintered bones and torn flesh, but often the bodies shifted under my weight and a spill of intestines and stomachs and livers and membranes would squirt out of the mass. More than once I had to stand on faces, and I felt teeth break under my heel.

My descent became more rapid when I stepped on a chest that buckled inwards with a wet snap of ribs, causing me to lose my balance and fall backwards onto the corpses, and ended up sliding-tumbling towards the bottom of the heap.

I slowly picked myself up, my clothes plastered to me with blood, blood slicking my hair to my forehead and making my face feel sticky. There were gashes and cuts and scrapes all over my body, and several tender spots were sure to bloom into bruises.

After I had made a cursory assessment of my physical state and concluded I was in good form when everything was considered, I turned my attention once more to my surroundings.

The train had levelled out enough to be a walking prospect again. Going forward was still a seemingly endless proposition, with windows measured out as precisely as before, and each row of seats all occupied by the corpses of versions of me which might have been, or were.

I turned back to the pile of corpses that Karen and I had caused.

Karen herself was not immediately apparent. She was not on the surface of the pile. This meant she was within the pile, and was almost certainly now dead, if not killed in the initial fall then certainly either crushed or suffocated.

But even in the face of this logic I felt the need to find her, to see her. Why? It was irrational, but for some reason I could not fully accept the irrefutable logic that stated she must be dead until I saw her corpse with my own eyes.

I grabbed a hand sticking out of the pile of dead

and pulled. Bodies shifted as I tugged free a version of me that had been covered in bread crumbs and deep fried. I or he or we smelled delicious.

I pulled the body further down the aisle and grabbed at a feathered foot, dragging an oily bird of prey me out of the heap. More bodies shifted, tumbled.

I kept going, kept pulling bodies out of the bloody heap, dragging them further down the aisle, heaping them into the laps of seated versions of me, stacking them up so I could go back and unearth more. And even as I did so, the bodies shifted, more tumbled down, and the pile of corpses seemingly renewed itself. How many were there? A hundred? Three hundred? They choked the train almost to the ceiling, so it was impossible to look up, to look back down the train and see if the pile was at least going down in any significant way.

I worked despite knowing full well the futility of the project. Even if my strength held out, even if I spent days working -days I could never count without an external way of tallying them- I knew the female version of me could not possibly be alive.

And still I worked.

In each row of seats, left and right, I stacked the bodies up and then moved up the train to the next row. Slowly I blocked off all the windows that looked onto darkness to a distance of nearly a quarter of a mile from the base of the corpse heap. I was covered in blood and sweat, staggering rather than walking, my arms aching and my legs trembling with the exertion of pulling bodies out, dragging them down the aisle, and then hoisting them into the laps of other corpses.

I suspected I was becoming delirious, but by this

point there was a feedback loop in my head; I knew my efforts were futile and that I should give up… but now I had already expended so much effort, to give up would prove how futile the exercise was. I had to see Karen's dead face to paradoxically justify the futility of my actions. There was no point in what I was doing, but to surrender without achieving my pointless goal was somehow even more pointless.

It was this semi-delirious state of mind that made me think that the movement I saw in the corpse heap on my next trip was simply the settling of disturbed bodies and nothing more. In fact, I was even dragging away yet another version of me -a tusked, cycloptic version of me- when the corpses rose and fell away from the version of me that had been hidden, huddling under them.

The robot me was tall, its head nearly brushing the train's ceiling. The uniform of black trousers, white T-shirt, and blue shirt were only torn wrappings around its bulk of intricate moving parts; cogs turned, pistons pumped, flywheels span, a mass of engineered brass, polished wood, ivory and tortoise shell.

It had been crouched down to form a protective shield over Karen, preventing the mass of bodies they were trapped under from suffocating her.

XVI
THEORIES

KAREN said the "steampunk" robot version of us was called Kelvin Swithun, and then she told me what steampunk was, which helped explain some of the more exotic materials he was built from. I had no pictures in my head of what a robot should look like, and had only the general notion that they were humanoid machines, but I had some expectations of what one should be like. I felt electricity should be involved somehow.

"It was amazing," said Karen. "He caught me. Then he crouched down over me so that the rest of the bodies wouldn't smash me to death and then… we got buried."

"And I Was Not Strong Enough To Dig Us Out," finished Kelvin. "Until The Burden Lightened."

His voice was odd. It was musical, like plucked strings, but it sounded recorded. It came from a face which was something like a very old-fashioned cash register mixed with a typewriter, with odd clock-face-like eyes.

"That was me," I said. "I moved the bodies, I was digging you out. I thought Karen might still be alive under there."

She grabbed me into an embrace, and then pressed her lips against my cheek.

"Thank you," she said. "I was running out of air. Kelvin could hold the bodies up, but they were packed so tightly no oxygen was getting in."

"It is amazing that he was there to catch you," I said.

Karen explained; first she had been falling, then she had felt Kelvin's giant metal and wood hands catch her. No sooner had he caught her than he had crouched over her, shielding her with his mechanical body as corpses hailed down. The fall had continued until they were completely covered with dead bodies, buried in cold flesh, and in the time they were buried they had gotten to know one another, his face tucked down into the pocket of air he had created for Karen to shelter in. She had told him about our journey heading up the train, and he had told her his story, which was much like ours.

Kelvin Swithun was an automaton, one of a race of robots who had been built, gained sentience, and taken over the world in the age of the industrial revolution.

Karen explained that was why she called him a "steampunk" robot. She said steampunk was a sub-genre of fantasy fiction set loosely around the age of industrial revolution, characterized by the existence of anachronistic technology, such as computers, or spaceships, or, in Kelvin's case, robots.

"We had time to chat, whilst I was waiting to run out of oxygen and die," Karen said.

"I Still Find It Hard To Accept That Machine

Consciousness Never Arose In Your Reality," said the robot us.

"I think it's close to happening," said Karen. "They've made computers that can beat Russian blokes at chess, and most people have given up thinking for themselves when their phones and tablets can do all that sort of thing for them."

I was excluded from participating in this discussion because I had no memory of a reality to call my own with which to compare with each of theirs. I found this sense of exclusion, though not a conscious decision of Karen and Kelvin's, to be an unwelcome and unpleasant experience.

Kelvin Swithun had found himself on board the train with no memory of how he had come to be here, so he had decided to explore his surroundings and find answers. He had set off in the direction that the corpses were all seated facing, going forwards, and had, he claimed, established the same rule of counting distance as myself and Karen had.

His experience was much the same as ours as well, noting that none of the corpses was identical to any other, and that though the variations between them ranged from the purely cosmetic through to the teratologically fabulous, he had come across no other like himself.

This was of course Karen's realization as well, and something that they had in common that excluded me. I was not so different from many if not most of the corpses. I was not unique as Karen and Kelvin were. The experience of being excluded was, once again, unpleasant, and even though I recognized that it was neither of their faults -as had their having realities to compare earlier in the conversation not been a conscious effort to exclude me- I still felt an irrational bitter anger towards them.

"…But When I Came To The Point Where I Could No Longer Move Forward," said Kelvin, "I Turned Around And Retraced My Steps. Eventually I Noticed The Ground Was Becoming Steeper, Until I Reached A Point Where I Would Have To Climb To Continue… Which Was When Karen Fell And I Caught Her."

"So, you all caught up Gav?" Karen asked me.

I shrugged. I was feeling petulant.

She either didn't notice or didn't care. She clapped her hands together.

"Right! Three heads have got to be better than one, so let's make ourselves a plan of action!"

"What Would You Suggest?" asked Kelvin.

"Well, we've already come a long way forward," said Karen. "And frankly, I don't like the idea of trying to negotiate the loop-the-loop we just came through, where I almost died…" she paused, considering. "Kelvin, I don't think it came up in our little chat under the bodies… exactly *what* was it that prevented you from going on, when you were heading up the train?"

"A Body," said the robot.

"A body?"

"Yes. It Was So Big It Choked The Entire Passage. I Could Not Get Around It."

"It was one of us? But massive?" asked Karen. "What else was it like? Was it flesh and blood or was it made of diamond or something?"

Kelvin's head turned to me.

"It Was Much The Same As Gavin Whiney In Every Particular Save Its Size."

"My name isn't Gavin," I snapped.

"Yes, it is, don't be an arse Gav," said Karen. She said this distractedly, her mind mostly on another topic. "I think… okay, maybe this is a bad idea, probably a disgusting one at least, but I think you should lead us to this body, Kelvin."

"May I Enquire As To Why?" he asked.

"Well, it's an obstacle, and obstacles are there to be overcome," she told him. "Or at least they are in stories."

"Ah, Yes, You're Theory That This Is Some Sort Of Metafictional Construct," said the robot. "As If We Are Each The Enoch Soames You Spoke Of. It Strikes Me As Unlikely, But With No Alternative Theory To Pursue, It At Least Affords A Direction To Strike Out In."

Karen giggled. I didn't like that giggle, though I couldn't place exactly what I disliked about it.

"You talk like somebody out of Sherlock Holmes!" she told the robot.

I didn't know who that was.

XVII
BETRAYAL

THEY compared universes as we journeyed onwards, him eating shirts to burn in his engine, and her stopping to nibble on my or hers or our cheese head, which sometimes was passed back to me to be chewed on but barely tasted.

I could not join in because I had no memories to compare with theirs.

We had passed nearly twenty corpses which were made of different cheeses. Karen had tasted each one, biting off a nose or an ear, nibbling on their cheeks, until she found once she liked best which she called "haloumi."

Even a universe where humans had evolved from processed dairy products would have been preferable to being as homeless as me. I bit out my tongue. It was salty and squeaky.

Kelvin Swithun worked as an adding machine for a fashion wholesaler, which Karen told him, from his description, sounded a lot like the tool wholesaler where she worked in accounts as a credit manager. They found laughter in this, that in her reality lawnmowers were tools whereas in his they were haute couture.

He lived with his partner and a half dozen pet Mexicans, which was unusual for, as he said, "Most Automata Still Treat Humans As Vermin." These and other parallels between their otherwise entirely divergent existences further served to alienate me.

They were almost walking hand in hand.

I had deliberately slowed my pace so as to fall behind, wondering how far ahead of me they would get before either realized my absence. As such most of their conversation became inaudible to me, so I was not prepared for what came next.

There was a half mile gap between us before Karen finally noticed that I had fallen behind.

She called, but I was too far away to hear what she said.

Karen and Kelvin stopped walking. I felt bitter but satisfied, and very slowly caught up to them.

Karen had her hands on her hips and was looking at me quizzically.

"Woolgathering, were we?" she asked when I rejoined them.

"I don't know what that means," I said. "I'm guessing that you don't mean it literally, owing to the absence of wool in our surroundings."

"You're learning! It means daydreaming, lost in your own thoughts."

"Yes," I said. "I was."

"Kelvin says we're about a mile away from the body."

I was disappointed she did not ask me the nature of the thoughts that had distracted me and caused me to lag so far behind.

The robot nodded.

"That Is Correct, We Will Arrive Presently."

"Good," I said.

I had an intuition there was a subtext. It was based on the way that the robot and the female me kept glancing at one another.

"What's going on?" I asked.

"Got a favor to ask," said Karen. "Actually, it's why we noticed you'd gotten so far behind, we turned around to ask you if it was cool… but you were way the Hell behind us. Which is a bit ironic, now I think about it."

Kelvin agreed.

"Yes, As That Was The Boon We Were Going To Crave Of You."

I was confused.

"I'm confused," I said.

Karen grinned.

"Well," she said, "it's weird -*really* weird- but then this whole situation is insane, so weirdness might be irrelevant now, but… me and Kelvin want to fuck."

The giant steam-powered robot us winced.

"That's A Crude Way Of Phrasing It."

"Jam off the bread," said Karen. She looked back at me. "So, we'd like a bit of privacy. I mean, yeah, it's weird wanting to fuck a robot version of myself, but it would be really weird if another me was watching."

"You want to have sex with him?" I asked.

"In a nutshell," said Karen, "turns out old Kelvin is a bit kinky too, said he'd always wondered what doing a human would be like…"

"In My Society, Such A Paraphilia Is Taboo."

"…and when am I ever going to get the chance to fuck a robot? See, if what Kelvin says about there being a body blocking the way up there is true, and if I'm right that it's an obstacle for us to overcome in some kind of metafictional story we're in, that means there's a big possible plot advancement coming, and who knows? Maybe it will lead us to getting out of here."

My emotions were an impossible mixture that boiled inside me, making me want to be sick, and I could only label the noxious brew with one word; betrayal. I didn't know how, or at least, could not rationalize why it felt that way -we had never verbalized fealty to one another, certainly- but there it was. She had betrayed me.

"You want to have sex with him?" I asked again.

"Yes. But it would be creepy if you were watching, so could you make yourself scarce for a bit? Just back up a mile or two, so you can't see us and we can't see you."

The next words out of my mouth were spoken without any conscious thought putting them there.

"But I could join in," I said.

Karen looked shocked.

"You fancy shagging a robot too?" she said. "Actually, seeing as though we're basically the same person that isn't…"

"I meant you," I said. "We could both do you at the same time."

Karen thought for a moment, possibly picturing the scene in her head, the possibilities. She looked at Kelvin.

"What do you think?"

"He Is Proposing A Three-Way Union," said the robot.

"I bloody know that!" she snapped. "I was asking…

you know what, never mind."

Karen grinned.

"Don't know why I didn't think of it myself," she said.

XVII
ORIFICES

KELVIN Swithun was more prodigiously endowed than myself.

We had cleared a space in the aisle and undressed. Our anatomies exposed, Karen had quickly cycled through a series of reactions to the exposed robot.

"*Bloody* hell!" she said, shocked. Then she laughed. "Oh, my god, Kelvin, you're as big as a bloody bull!" She laughed again. "A mechanical bull!" Then she was shocked once more. "How the fuck are you going to fit that inside me?"

"I Would Assume Via Your Front Access Slot," he said.

His penis was the size of my forearm, a brass piston sheathed in leather foreskin, its glans a fist-sized piece of carved whalebone. Standing proud, it came up as far as Karen's throat. She reached out one tentative hand and ran her fingers along its length.

She coughed.

"You're going to need to lube this thing up," she said.

"Ah, Yes, Animals Have Soft Tissues And Membranes Which Are Easily Torn. I Understand. Unfortunately, Though, There Are No Oils Or Unguents Immediately To Hand, So How Do You Propose We Proceed?"

"I dunno," she said. "If me and Paul get fruity and can't lay our mitts on baby oil, he normally just spits in his fist."

"Very Well," said the robot. It opened its cash register mouth and a small spigot slid out. It cupped one palm underneath to catch about a pint of pale amber fluid. It used this to grease the length of its enormous organ.

Karen sniffed the air. Behind her, naked and ignored, I also smelled the air. It smelled quite pleasant, in an unpleasant way. Karen had a name for it.

"Is that petrol?" she asked.

"Petroleum Distillate," agreed Kelvin, "Yes. I Am A Hybrid, And I Am Not Ashamed Of That Fact!"

His tone and words combined to suggest a whole alternate history with its own complex culture of social norms, customs, and prejudices. His cock glistened with all the colors of a sickened rainbow.

Karen was holding her hands up.

"Sorry, sorry! Didn't mean to imply anything, I was just asking!" Then she turned herself to the practicalities of the situation. "Right. Here's what I think; the good old trying for a bishop, you lying on the floor, me straddling you, and…" She turned to me. "Gav, you can take me up the chocolate chimney."

"Excuse me?" I asked, perplexed. I was trying to understand what "trying for a bishop" meant and then she had said something about chocolate and chimneys. "What do you mean?"

"I Believe Karen Is Employing A Colourful Euphemism For Her Rectum," said Kelvin.

"…and make sure you lube up as well," said Karen. "You might not be a mechanical bull but I'm not taking nine inches up the bum bone dry, either. Come on, let's get this done and then get onto the next plot twist."

The machine man lay down on his back in the aisle, brass and leather cock standing tall and proud.

"Like This?" he asked.

Karen blew out her cheeks.

"Jesus, if I slip I'll turn into a kebab. Here, give me a little of that," she said, using her fingers to strip some of the rainbow coloured fluid from Kelvin's penis, fingers which slipped into her pussy. "Ahh! Cold!"

She stood with her legs outspread, her hands bracing against the chairs on either side of the aisle, and slowly squatted down. The whalebone glans stretched the lips of her vagina wide, and very carefully she began to sink down onto him. She was biting her lower lip and her eyes were closed tightly. A low, strained sound came from deep in her throat.

When she was halfway down she stopped and gasped.

"That's it, no more," said Karen. "It feels like I'm trying to stuff a fire extinguisher wrapped in belts up my twat! Jesus! Gav? You ready?"

I was. For some reason, even though I had been jealous of the intimacy enjoyed by the female me and the steampunk robot me, I found the sight of them coupled had filled me with lust, and that my own erection stood true and solid in front of me. I spat in my palm and baptized the length of myself. The sensation caused a jolt of pleasure and my penis twitched.

"Oh god, what have I let myself in for?" said Karen, half moaning and half laughing. She adjusted her grip on the chairs and lifted herself a few inches, then lowered herself again. She repeated this a few times. "Okay, I can just about… how's that for you Kelvin?"

"It Feels… Remarkable," said the robot.

"That's one way of putting it," said Karen, grinning. "Gav, go slowly, yeah?"

I wasn't sure I would be able to. My head felt stuffed and confused and all I wanted to do was ram myself into her as hard and as deep as I could, over and over until the frustration blasted out of me.

I swallowed thickly.

"Okay," I told her, and nestled the purple bulb of my glans between the round white globes of her bottom. I gripped myself by the root and slid down until I found her anus, and into this I gradually eased myself, the whole length of my erection seeming to thrum with anticipation.

Karen's anus was incredibly tight. At first I thought I would not be able to force myself in, but then I heard and felt her gasp, willing muscles to relax, and gradually I begin to fill her. The tightness wasn't just the natural clenching of her sphincter, I realized; the act of taking so much of Kelvin's cock up into her pussy meant there was very little room left within the secret cavities of her body. I could feel his hardness barely separated from me by internal muscle and membrane, and another thrill ran through me.

"Hmmnnnnn," Karen moaned. "Jesus, did you grow another six inches when I wasn't looking?"

"No. That wouldn't be physically possible," I told

her, but -no matter how impossible her statement- for some reason it pleased me, and I found myself thrusting harder into her.

"*Fuck!* Careful! Stop, stop Gav!"

I didn't want to, but then she was glaring over her shoulder at me. I paused.

"Right, we need some coordination here guys," she said. "Just let me set the rhythm, you two follow along, and try not to get too excited too early, because if you blow your loads before I'm even halfway there I will be royally cheesed off. Right?"

"I Will Comply," said Kelvin.

My cock twitched, but my hips stayed still. That was my assent.

"Right," said Karen. Her knuckles whitened as she gripped the backs of the chairs even tighter. "One, two, three…"

XIX
BURROWING

FOR the second time in my limited existence I was about to breach an anus.

Our three-way sex session hadn't lasted long, as we discovered that we were all in a heightened state of arousal, and that not much effort was required in order for each one of us to orgasm. Karen had done so twice before either Kelvin or I did, and for reasons which weren't clear to me I was pleased that the steampunk robot had "blown his load" before me. Not long before, but still, I felt what Karen later identified for me as "pride" at having outlasted him.

The force of Kelvin's orgasm, combined with the sheer quantity of material that he ejaculated, forced Karen off his cock -which was, as she put it, "like trying to sit on a firehose at full blast"- nearly lifting her from her feet and almost off my erection. She lost her grips on the chair backs, and just before the tip of my penis slid free of her rectum she fell backwards into my lap, sending us both sprawling to the floor. The sudden impact plunged me all the way to the root of my cock into her insides, and then I finally came, flooding her anus with semen.

Karen was the first to her feet sometime later. She got up slowly, using a nearby corpse filled chair for support until she stood on her unsteady legs. Her thighs were streaked black with the material that Kelvin had ejaculated into her, flooding out of her vagina and down her legs.

"Right, I think I can cross a lot of stuff off my bucket list," she said. "I feel like someone has cunt punted me for a fortnight, and my bum is burning like the morning after a prawn vindaloo."

She farted a streamer of speckled brown semen. Then she queefed what must have been a pint of the viscous black material the robot had pumped into her.

She slid her fingers inside herself to scrape out the remainder. She sniffed them afterwards.

"Smells like coal tar soap," she said.

"That's Because It *Is* Coal Tar," said Kelvin.

"That's… really gross."

"And Anything Human's Produce Is Better?"

Karen made use of the clothes of various corpses to clean herself up. Kelvin and I followed suit, careful not to look at one another. For some reason, even though we had just shared an act of extreme intimacy, I felt a curious mixture of shame and self-loathing. Karen would later explain that this was normal, and was called embarrassment. As I dressed, my mind kept returning to the sensation of the steampunk robot's cock inside Karen, pressing up against my own erection through the thin membranous walls of her innards, and each time the thought came around I felt heat flood my face.

We spoke little as we continued onwards. I wondered if the others felt as I did, and decided that they must do. Even though Karen complained about how sore she was, she stayed in front, moving briskly, occasionally asserting over her shoulder that she knew things would change once we reached the giant corpse that Kelvin had spoken of.

I had my doubts about her belief that we were somehow fictional characters, though I had no alternative theory to offer. The story she had used to define the genre of metafiction was about one man called Max Beerbohm and another called Enoch Soames. Karen said the story wasn't written as a story, but as a personal account of the writer, Beerbohm, of what had befallen another writer he knew, the man Soames. Soames was obsessed with being remembered long after his death. He made a deal with the Devil; his soul in exchange for a day in a library one hundred years in the future. During this time he searched for his books, or for any mention of them, or himself, wanting to know if he was remembered. He found nothing until it was almost time to leave, when he discovered a reference to himself as being a character in a short story written by Beerbohm. Upon returning to his own time he berated Beerbohm for portraying him as nothing but a character in a short story, before the Devil whisked him away and the whole thing became "a self-fulfilling prophecy".

What Karen was proposing was that we were all Enoch Soames. My problem was, if this were true, who was the writer? Who was our Beerbohm, and what was the point of all this?

Karen didn't have answers to these questions, but believed they involved overcoming the obstacle of the giant corpse. Her belief seemed as strong as iron, but with every mile she seemed to grow ever more manic. When we caught sight of the enormous body that was blocking the train she began to lope towards it as fast as her abused flesh would allow, laughing and calling for us to follow, hurry, come on slowpokes, let's go. Kelvin and I followed.

The corpse was lying on its front, back pressed tight against the ceiling, chest and belly crushing the ranks of seats. The soles of its huge feet were towards us, lying on top of the backrests of seats which had not broken under the weight, so that the aisle lead up between its splayed legs to the seat of its trousers.

This was where Karen had stopped.

She turned, grinning.

"Look at the size of that arse!" she cried.

"So, You See The Problem," said Kelvin. "Our Progress Ends Here As There Is Simply No Way Around, Over, Or Underneath. That Is Why I Turned Back."

"Yes, Kelvin, I understand," said Karen, but she was still grinning.

"What are you thinking?" I asked. Her grin was putting me on edge. It was more like she was baring her teeth than showing genuine happiness.

"If we can't go over it, and we can't go under it," she said slowly, "and we can't go around it, then we simply have to go *straight through it*."

She produced a shard of broken pottery and turned

to the seat of the trousers. She slashed at the fabric with the sharp edge of her improvised knife, and cut a foot-long gash. Into this she reached, securing a grip on either ragged edge, and ripped it wider, extending the gash vertically with short, hard tugs.

When she was finished, she had made a gap big enough for the corpse's buttocks to show through. These she pushed apart, to expose a puckered, stained-brown anus.

"The chocolate chimney," I said.

"That's right Gav, well done!" said Karen. "Up the bum, through the guts, into the belly, then straight up the throat and out over the lips!"

Kelvin's face of stops and keys and dials arranged itself into an expression of disgust.

"The Very Notion Is Revolting!" he declared. "Forcing Myself Inside A Human!"

"Oh really?" said Karen slyly. "And what were we all doing not so long ago? Our little gangbang back there? You were happy enough to force yourself inside a human then."

The robot protested.

"But This Is A Different Scenario Entirely!"

"Really? Go on then, explain, how is jamming yourself into me different then what I'm proposing now?"

"Two Variables Are Vastly Different," said the robot us. "The Quantity Of My Body And The Express Purpose; I Only Placed 5% Of My Total Mass Inside You As Opposed To 100% Here, And The Express Purpose Formerly Was That Of Mutual Gratification, Whereas Now It's…"

"…the possibility of escaping whatever the fuck this

situation is, and maybe getting back to our respective realities?" Karen interrupted. "Which of those would you deem more important?

Kelvin found himself without an argument to make.

"I Concede The Point," he said.

Karen looked at me.

"How about it Gav?"

I regarded the dirty orifice of the colossal version of us.

"I don't think we have much choice," I said.

Karen sighed.

"There's nothing like a little enthusiasm," she said, "...and that was nothing like a little enthusiasm!"

I looked at the anus. It smelled of shit.

"Come on! This could be our ticket out of here!" she said, and so saying she placed her hands together as if praying or preparing to dive, and pushed them into our arsehole.

XX
AN ENDING

THIS book is almost done now, each page of skin filled with the memories of the early times, penned in our blood, to tell the senseless generations to come of how everything began, though they will never understand or care. Karen warned me long ago, before she died, that it was important that they know that things could be, and were, different elsewhere.

Our offspring, and theirs in turn, cannot conceive of "elsewhere". I can barely do so, and I heard of such dreams from the mouths of two who had memories, and I at least started with a fully stocked mind, even if I lacked the experiences to account for my knowledge.

Reading, writing; I have tried to teach these to our offspring, but they do not care. They would rather fuck and feast.

I am very old now. How old I do not know, as we never could find a way of marking time. I look in the windows, at my reflection floating on the darkness, and

I see my hair is mostly gone and my flesh is deeply troughed with wrinkles. My eyes are filmy and sunken, my teeth nearly all gone. I am bent and frail, and my organs are withering within me.

So.

We crawled and we dug and somehow, we pushed through, somehow, we penetrated the giant corpse, emerging from its mouth like bloody vomit.

What did we see?

The train carried on, just as before. There was no plot twist, no revelation, no escape.

Karen never lost her belief that things would change, even if Kelvin and myself quietly agreed, as time passed, that this was our reality now. We continued onwards only in search of resources, plundered from the infinite variations of our corpses. Karen and I ate of versions of us made from every kind of food, whilst Kelvin made use of the clothing as fuel for his internal combustion engine.

We came across many grotesque sights, and many marvels, versions of us who could have on

The body of the train changed, though there was no obvious pattern to how or when these changes might occur. There were sometimes loops, though these were more easily navigated than that first had been, with Kelvin's assistance. There were sections that turned sharp corners, or zig-zagged; there were gentle slopes, near-vertical drops, sections stuffed with giants or filled with versions of us that were so outlandish in form that we had to negotiate labyrinths of weird flesh.

The materials and dimensions around us never changed. The regular gaps between the windows, and the emptiness beyond those windows, never changed.

We walked, we slept, we ate, we fucked.

Sometimes we stopped for long periods. It was during one such long rest that we were briefly able to measure time, though ultimately it had no relevance; Karen explained that a pregnancy lasted nine months, and so she wanted us to remain in a particularly well-stocked section, because she would be eating for two and would probably develop some strange habits.

"My mum always said," she explained, "that when she was preggers with me she had a hankering for pilchards on Mars bars. She'd have a tin of pilchards in tomato sauce, and she'd have as many Mars bars as my dad could buy from Mr. Shah's shop down the road, and she'd sit there of an evening watching TV and eating pilchard topped Mars bars."

Many of these words meant nothing to me, but we had time in abundance, and so all her life, and that of the steampunk robot called Kelvin Swithun, would become known to me with every proper noun explained.

The section of the train Karen had desired to "nest" in had a dozen versions of us who were vending machines, a few of which dispensed more than just food; one was filled with toys, tiny action figure versions of ourselves, though I only recognized two as being specimens whose corpses we had directly observed.

During her pregnancy, Karen was no longer sexually available, so Kelvin and I found ourselves relying more on each other for gratification, though she would watch and offer her thoughts on the various positions we tried whilst gobbling aubergines the size of grapes smeared on top of candy bars whose wrappers identified them as *Covefefe Cheewees*.

Our first child was a girl.

We taught her to walk. We taught her to read and to write, skinning corpses and drying the flesh to use as parchment, using fingers bones dipped in blood for ink. As we taught her, so we developed techniques of rendering different kinds of bodies for different purposes, which she learned along with us; we fashioned tools from dead usses.

As time passed our family grew. The incest was inevitable, as we couldn't keep a track of them all; sometimes a pair or a trio of our offspring would leave, various combinations of brother and sisters, travelling up or down the train, and we would encounter them later, with offspring of their own, each new tribe having variations on the survival techniques we had developed, new customs, new traditions.

One large tribe attacked us late in our lives. The leader, my son with my first daughter, ambushed us as we slept; he had assembled half a dozen different tribes of children under his command, with the ultimate aim of overthrowing we three who were their parents. They dismantled Kelvin piece by piece and forced me to watch as my first son raped his own mother. I thought he would kill me, for he had never seemed to like me, even as an infant, but he did not. He had established himself as the dominant force on the train for a thousand miles in either direction, and I was bound as a prisoner.

Karen died trying to give birth to something so misshapen it tore her in two.

And so finally I alone remained of we three who

knew or cared about a reality outside this train. I am permitted to write, though I no longer know why I bother, as none of the offspring care to learn to read. This is one skill that has been lost, and yet I acquire skins and dry them, and then I take blood and I write down everything I can remember of the stories that Karen and Kelvin told me, and this account of where it all started.

The offspring do not care. They all look like me but they are little more than animals, eating corpses, ever moving forward, up the train towards no known destiny, walking and feasting and fucking, always surrounded by the infinite corpses of us.

XX
ANOTHER ENDING

I have spent the past twenty minutes reading up on how to cook eggplant, trying to decide what to do with the fruit I purchased on impulse at the Armenian grocer down the block from my apartment.

It is a fruit, sitting there on the counter all shiny and plump, even if we treat it like a vegetable. Like tomatoes, those are fruit too, berries in fact, and related to the eggplant. We treat tomatoes like vegetables as well.

Even as I think these thoughts, they sound false, hollow. As if they are not mine. As if they are being written by someone, somewhere, and I am just an actor repeating them inside the theater of my head, for an audience of one; me.

I've felt this way since we crawled through the dead giant. Something went wrong and I almost suffocated inside it. They pulled me out, resuscitated me, and it was to a scattering of applause and some relieved laughter that I came too on the stage, lying with my head being cradled by the stage hand who had been blowing *Grape Drank* vape flavored breath into me.

"Thought we'd lost you, man! Was near damn sure we had!"

I struggled to sit up, and several other members of the production crowded around to help me.

Of course right then I didn't know who they were, except for Karen and Kelvin. Except Kelvin didn't look much like Kelvin, but more like a man in a costume. And Karen wasn't Karen either.

I am an actor. More specifically, I am a method actor. I take weeks to prepare for a role, spending that time getting inside the head of the character I am going to play, learning them inside out, getting right inside their skin and into the wet-electric coils of their brain. For all intents and purposes, I become that character. My immersion is so full-on that, for the period of the play's run on stage, it becomes my entire reality. This intensity, given to every performance, has made me one of the most talked about actors of the past twenty years. I have appeared in such diverse stage productions as Samuel Beckett's *End Game,* Sarah Kane's *Blasted,* and Cormac McCarthy's *The Sunset Limited.* I have won two Tony awards, and have even written and directed a play of my own, a play featuring every person present on the album cover of The Beatle's *Seargent Pepper's Lonely Hearts Club Band* as a character.

These are all facts that have been related to me by the rest of the company. These are the facts of my reality now, and I accept them, even if I do not wholly believe them… as my own memory of life before the train has not returned.

I was rehearsing a play called *Genocide on the Infinite Express* when I got into difficulty inside the prop of a giant corpse. A stage hand had pulled me out and resuscitated me, and the intense state of concentration I had entered into had finally shattered; I became aware that the train was not in fact a sealed tube of infinite length, but in fact was open on one side, the side where the audience would be sat in ranks of tattered red seats, watching.

I became aware that there were more than just three of us in existence, and that these other two usses were in fact not variations of me, but two other actors. It seems as though I am having an affair with the woman who plays Karen Swainey. Her husband knows about the affair; he is a psychotherapist who specialises in treating people with eating disorders. He has written a book on diabulimia, a form of bulimia affecting people with diabetes, who utilise their need of regular injections of the hormone insulin as a dangerous method of losing weight.

His "thing" is being cuckolded. On occasion, he has watched.

I have taken my time in looking around this apartment, in carefully examining the traces of a life lived, attempting to understand who I apparently am by the things I have chosen to fill my personal space. There are a number of masks on one wall of the bedroom, perhaps enough of them to be considered a collection. The bed in is made up for one person; the mattress is made of a kind of memory foam.

There is no TV.

I keep returning to the kitchen and the eggplant, the only thing I have bought for reasons beyond simple survival since my accident at the rehearsal. I mean, I've bought food, but only with a view to providing my body with fuel, so it has always been just snacks and canned sodas. An eggplant is something that needs to be prepared. I wonder if I am a good cook. Do I know how to prepare this strange vegetable that is really a fruit? If my memory comes back to me, will there be recipes employing eggplant amongst them? Perhaps I bought it based on an instinct; maybe I often cook with eggplant, or *aubergine*, and in fact know of many, many ways of preparing it; roasted, grilled, fried (in olive oil, in extra virgin olive oil, in coconut oil, in ghee), served with linguine or fusilli or ravioli pasta, with cheese (Parmesan? Halloumi?), with jerked goat or turkey vindaloo, as an entrée, or a side, so many different ways of cooking it, so many other ingredients to pair it with, possibly an endless number of possible dishes rotating around the same plump, glossy, purple berry.

I am the eggplant man.

XX
YET ANOTHER ENDING

NOW we had cans of soup instead of heads.

Karen had been wrong. We had dug our way through the corpse, emerging from between its lips, to discover that nothing was any different. The train was the same, and it was still filled with corpses. Only now these dead versions of us had cans of soup instead of heads. In every other regard they were exactly the same as me, but their necks grew into giant metal cans bearing paper wrappers that declared the brand name of the company that had made them, the name of the kind of soup contained within, and a picture of that kind of soup. Also on the label were a list of ingredients, as well as instructions on how to heat the soup.

Every flavor was different, but the brand name was always the same. Karen explained the concept of "brand names" to me, though she didn't know why some of the soups had names that extended beyond a basic description of the main ingredient, like French Onion,

Bird's Nest, Cream of Mushroom, or Sharks Fin. She did not know why Cullen Skink, Mulligatawny, Tom Yum, Alphabet, She-Crab, Gazpacho, Brown Windsor, Egg-Drop, Snert, Philadelphia Pepper Pot, Callaloo, Primordial, or Cock-a-leekie soup were called what they were called. And there were others which she did not recognize at all, deducing they must be flavors of soup eaten in corners of the multiverse that did not bear thinking about; Pinkeye, Cigarette-Butt, Chicken & Chyme, Smegma.

In fact, when I asked her what the significance of each of these names were, she replied in the same flat monotone of voice that she did not know, and she did not care.

I made a deductive leap of reasoning that her defeated demeanor was a result of having discovered that she was wrong in assuming our situation would change once we had made our passage through the giant corpse of ourself.

Kelvin had become curious as to the contents of the cans and using his robotic strength had peeled the lid from a version of us who had a can of Carrot & Coriander soup for a head.

Inside the can was full of carrot and coriander soup, but not only that. Kelvin gently tipped the corpse forward to allow a quantity of the creamy orange fluid to pour out onto the floor, and having done so revealed that there was a brain and naked eyes, attached to the brain by optical nerves, floating in the soup.

I opened my mouth to make an observation, but instead of words issuing forth I found myself belching, which quickly turned into retching, which finally turned into vomiting.

I vomited three small versions of us and an incredible amount of bloody tissue. Their bodies were so big that they pushed out all of my front teeth as they emerged, and the corners of my mouth split, ripping my cheeks.

I collapsed to the ground next to them. Apparently, significant damage had been done to my insides.

My head had landed next to the three small versions of myself who were picking themselves up and attempting to remove as much gore as possible. Sloughing off sheaths of stomach lining and bloody mucous, they revealed themselves to be a tiny version of myself, a tiny version of Karen, and a tiny version of Kelvin.

I heard Karen say "What the fuck?" at exactly the same moment that the tiny version of herself also said "What the fuck?"

Then the small version of me began to vomit. He vomited three tiny versions of myself, Karen, and Kelvin, or perhaps they were tiny versions of the small versions of ourselves.

…and then that tiny version began to vomit…

I could only assume that a shrinking waterfall of puke would continue cascading down to the atomic level, carrying ever decreasing versions of myself into unknown and unknowable territory. I do not know, for whatever damage was wrought within me by that first vomited trio was fatal, and I died.

XX
THE ENDING

Fucking pile of wank.

I sat back in my chair and looked at the last thing I'd written.

"Come on! This could be our ticket out of here!" she said, and so saying she placed her hands together as if praying or preparing to dive, and pushed them into our arsehole.

I had no idea what came next.

To be fair, I had no idea what was going to happen in any chapter, as the story was just an experiment, to take a weird central image of a train full of corpses and just run with it. But then I'd broken the fourth wall too early, and now I was buried under the rubble.

Shit metaphor. Fuck it.

Why? Nobody liked meta-fiction. Except me. Well, maybe some people did. But not many. For most people it just made them angry. Most people just wanted a story that had a beginning, a middle, and an end, a self-contained narrative they could get lost in for a while before returning to the narrative they each called their own life.

AND NEVER THE TWAIN SHALL MEET MOTHERFUCKER.

So now I was wondering how to end it. Because this had to be the end. The three protagonists were about to pass through a body, an event which one of them had already declared must be a pivotal moment in the plot.

An ending.

It had to be good. Or at least original. The average consumer of media in this day and age was so savvy they could see almost every twist ending coming. So, it could not "all be just a dream", because that had become a tired cliché before the phrase "tired cliché" had itself become a tired cliché.

Maybe they discovered they were in Hell?

No, that had already been done.

Maybe the story could twist around on itself, start at the beginning again in a loop.

No, that had been done. In fact, both had been done, invented in fact, by the same writer, in the same book, *The Third Policeman* by Flann O'Brien.

Fuck it.

I decided to write a few different endings, and let the reader decide which they preferred. We lived in an ultra-capitalist society where having a wide variety of choices was more important than quality; why shouldn't our fiction have reflected this? Many movies had alternate endings, and multiple different outcomes to the main narrative was pretty much standard in modern videogames. And besides, I'd always wanted to try a mindfuck whose logistics had meant it was almost impossible; to write a book where every single edition was different from every other, sometimes in a small way, such as a single line of dialogue, right through to something huge… like the ending.

So, I needed to come up with a few different outcomes to this story. I decided to clear my head by having a wank. At my desk, screen before me waiting to fill it up with strings of semantically empty symbols, I mused.

I am thirty-six years old. If we say puberty started at the age of eleven -which is to say, masturbation began to produce viable sperm- and on average I battered myself silly at least once a day, that would give us nine thousand one hundred and twenty-five separate acts of self-abuse (or wet dreams, or, as I grew up and began to engage with the opposite gender, other various acts.) The average human ejaculation contains two hundred and fifty million sperm. So, in all, that's two trillion, two hundred and eighty-one billion, two hundred and fifty million individual little white tadpoles that have come out of me. Every single one of those could have been a person. According to multiverse theory, every single one of those has become a person. But not here, not in this universe, where instead they ended up drying on my bedsheets, or in a rubber sheath tossed down the toilet, or were digested by obliging partners.

Every blowjob, a genocide.

I came on the keyboard. The orgasm was fast and joyless and almost immediately following my "little death" I was disgusted with the sticky ivory fluid cooling on the clustered plastic islands of the alphabet. "Little death"; such an elegant way of putting it. I yawned, mentally comparing that French turn of phrase with the various English idioms for what I had ejaculated;

spunk, spaff, cock-hock, dick-spittle, filthy concrete, people paste, population porridge, man-mayo, guy-goo, Valentine's Day mascara.

I think I'll just rest my eyes for a bit.

I fell asleep at the keyboard.

I had a strange dream.

Or maybe I died in my sleep.

There were... there are...

Corpses everywhere, not all of them human, but all of them me.

ABOUT THE AUTHOR

Kevin Sweeney is the author of DAMNATION 101 (Strangehouse Books), THE WHOREHOUSE THAT JACK BUILT (MorbidbookS), MONSTER COOKIES (KHP) and SIDESHOW P.I. (with Nathaniel Lambert, Graveside Tales.) and a bunch of others. I used to spend a lot of time in Bangkok. He breed chihuahuas and shire horses with his wife on Loch Ness.